A SERPENT OF SATAN

The Earl thought that the room had suddenly been lit with a thousand candles as Ophelia's eyes met his.

With a little murmur she moved towards him and hid her face against his shoulder.

"I must be dreaming," she whispered. "I did not even . . . dare to pray that you would . . . love me."

The Earl turned her face up to his.

"When we have a little more time, I will tell you exactly how much I care."

He bent his head as he spoke and his lips found hers. He could not imagine that any woman's mouth could be so soft, so yielding and yet so exciting.

And for Ophelia it was as if he filled the whole world, the earth and the sky, and she knew this was the moment she had been waiting for.

"I . . . love you. I love you," she whispered.

The Earl gazed at her reverently.

"And I love you, my darling!"

Bantam Books by Barbara Cartland
Ask your bookseller for the books you have missed

Barbara Cartland's Library of Love series

Barbara Cartland's Ancient Wisdom series

Other Books by Barbara Cartland

Barbara Cartland
A Serpent of Satan

A SERPENT OF SATAN
A Bantam Book | April 1979

ISBN 0-553-12637-7

Published simultaneously in the United States and Canada

Bantam Books are published by Bantam Books, Inc. Its trade-
mark, consisting of the words "Bantam Books" and the por-
trayal of a bantam, is Registered in U.S. Patent and Trademark
Office and in other countries. Marca Registrada. Bantam
Books, Inc., 666 Fifth Avenue, New York, New York 10019.

Author's Note

The second Earl of Rochester (1647–80) was the most notorious of the Restoration Rakes. He was also an outstandingly lyrical and satirical poet.

His life of lechery, wild pranks, dialogues, and practical-jokes brought him the punishment of being exiled from Court, but King Charles remained his friend and even joined in some of his erotic escapades.

His friend Etherege depicted him in the Stage-Character "Dorimant"—"I know he is a Devil, but he has something of the Angel yet undefac'd in him."

A Serpent of Satan

Chapter One

1802

The Earl of Rochester drew his four horses to a standstill with an expertise which brought a look of admiration to his groom's face.

"Walk them, Jason!" he ordered as he stepped down from his Phaeton.

His man had already rung the bell which hung outside the heavy porticoed doors of Lord Langstone's house in Park Lane.

The door was opened immediately by a footman wearing a blue livery trimmed with yellow, which were the Langstone colours.

The Earl knew the colours well, for Lord Langstone often competed with him on the race-course, where the Earl was invariably the winner, as he was in every other sport he undertook.

If his groom looked at him with admiration, so did the other flunkeys who stood in the marble Hall of the Langstone mansion.

There is nothing the English admire more than a sportsman, and to the racing-public the Earl was predominately the "King of Sport," while in other activities he excelled in a different manner, which was usually spoken of in whispers.

As the Butler came hurrying towards him, the Earl asked in his habitual drawl:

"Is Her Ladyship in?"

"Yes, M'Lord. I'll inform Her Ladyship of your arrival."

The Butler went ahead up the curved staircase, which had been climbed by many distinguished people, and

led the Earl into the long Drawing-Room which
stretched the whole length of the house.

It was a room that seemed to have been made for
entertaining. The crystal chandeliers caught the sunshine coming through the windows, while the hot-house
flowers, doubtless from Lord Langstone's Estate in the
country, filled the air with fragrance.

The Earl walked languidly across the carpet, and
only as the Butler closed the door behind him did he
realise that he was not alone.

In a far corner of the room, intent on arranging some
flowers in a vase, was a young woman.

Only when he actually reached the centre of the
room was she aware of his presence. She turned to
look at him with an expression in her eyes which, to
his surprise, was one of fear.

The Earl was used to receiving every sort of glance
from women of every age, but fear was not included;
in fact the most common was one of adoration.

Yet he realised now that the girl—for she was little
more—was extremely disturbed by his presence.

Hastily she picked up the flowers that she had not yet
placed in the vase and started to move away from the
side-table in an obvious effort to reach the door.

To do so, however, she had to pass the Earl, and as
she came near to him he saw that she had an unusual
loveliness which he could not remember ever seeing
before.

She was also very young, seventeen or eighteen, his
experienced eye estimated, and she was dressed in a
simple gown that was slightly out of fashion.

Her small waist was encircled with a blue sash.

"Perhaps I should introduce myself," he said as she
came to a standstill a few feet from him.

"I know who . . . you are, My Lord," she murmured
uncomfortably. "And I . . . I should not be here. I am
. . . afraid . . . I m-misjudged the time."

"I think in actual fact I am early," the Earl said,
which he knew was the truth.

He had driven his horses at such a speed round the
Park that he had arrived at his destination at least

twenty minutes ahead of the time at which he had told Lady Langstone to expect him.

"I . . . I must . . . go."

The words were hardly above a whisper, but he heard them, and he deliberately moved two steps so that he stood directly in the route which the girl wished to take.

"Before you leave," he said, "as you are obviously aware of my identity, it is only fair that I should know yours."

She looked up at him and the fear was back in her eyes.

As if she felt compelled to reply, she said:

"I am . . . Ophelia Langstone . . . My Lord."

"Are you telling me that you are Lord Langstone's daughter?" the Earl enquired.

"Yes . . . My Lord."

"By his first marriage, of course?"

"Yes . . . My Lord."

"Then I suppose your Stepmother will be presenting you this Season? Or are you still at School?"

There was an obvious pause. Then with a little tremor in her voice Ophelia replied:

"I . . . I shall . . . not be presented . . . My Lord!"

The Earl raised his eye-brows. At the same time, knowing Lady Langstone, he thought it very unlikely that she would wish to chaperone a stepdaughter, and certainly not one who was so lovely.

Ophelia glanced towards the door, then at the Earl.

He waited, thinking that her beauty was something which seemed to belong not to the present but to the past.

She had nothing in common with the fashionable, full-blown Junoesque type of beauty set by Georgina, Duchess of Devonshire, twenty years ago, or the mature attractions of Mrs. Fitzherbert.

There was something classical in the little oval face with its straight nose and perfectly curved lips, and there was also, he thought, a spiritual look which he had not expected to see in such a young girl.

The Earl was a connoisseur of women, just as he was

a superb judge of horse-flesh and an epicure when it came to food and wine.

He found himself wondering now where he had last seen such a face or a grace such as hers, which had attracted his attention from the moment she began to cross the room.

He realised that she had something to say to him, and now once again, glancing at the door as if she was afraid of who might open it, she said in a voice that was hardly above a whisper:

"May I . . . ask Your Lordship . . . something?"

"Of course," the Earl replied, wondering what she was about to say to him.

"Do you . . . remember Jem Bullet?"

The Earl knitted his brows together.

The name seemed familiar, but he could not place it.

"Jem Bullet!" he repeated.

"He was a jockey in your . . . employ some . . . years ago."

"Of course!" he exclaimed. "Jem Bullet! A good rider. He won several races for me."

"Then could you not do . . . something for him . . . now?"

The Earl definitely frowned.

"Do something for him?" he repeated. "I recall that he left my employment."

"He had an accident!"

"Yes, of course!" the Earl said. "I remember now. He had an accident. I retired him."

"Without a . . . pension!"

"That is not true!"

The Earl's voice was sharp.

"I have never in my life, Miss Langstone, and this is the truth, retired a man or a woman who has served me well, without ensuring their future."

"But not . . . Jem Bullet," Ophelia replied.

Now there was a note in her voice that told the Earl she was criticising him.

He opened his lips to expostulate, but as he did so, there was a sound outside the door, and the girl standing in front of him started.

In a voice he could hardly hear, she said:

"Please ... please ... do not tell ... Stepmama that I have ... spoken to you."

There was a cry of sheer, undiluted fear. Then, with the swiftness of a fawn, before the door could open she had reached it, as if she was on the point of leaving the room.

But it was not the person she feared who stood there. It was only the Butler.

Ophelia passed him without a word and vanished down the passage.

"Her Ladyship asks, M'Lord," the Butler said to the Earl, "if you would be gracious enough to join her in her *Boudoir*."

It was what the Earl had expected, and he merely walked back across the room, and the Butler went ahead of him down the passage.

The Earl found himself looking to see if there was any further sign of Ophelia, but there was only the quietness of the large house and the heavy footsteps of the Butler ahead of him.

"Jem Bullet!"

The Earl said the name beneath his breath, remembering now the small, wizened little man whose way with horses had invariably taken them first past the winning-post.

He recalled the accident. He had been disappointed to learn that it was unlikely that Jem Bullet would be able to ride again.

But of course he had provided for him, as he always did for those who had served him well.

He wondered how Ophelia Langstone could have received such inaccurate information, and why in any case she should concern herself with other people's servants.

Thinking of her, he realised that he knew very little about the Langstones except that Lady Langstone had been pursuing him for some time.

It was nothing new for the Earl to be pursued by the type of woman she undoubtedly was, but it was a relief to know that the mothers of eligible daughters felt that he was to be avoided at all costs.

He had had quoted at him so often the words which had described the man he emulated: "A Devil with something of the Angel yet undefac'd in him."

He would therefore have been somewhat disconcerted had he been accepted in what he thought of to himself as "Polite Society."

Only his very closest friends, and they were few, knew what a complex character the Earl actually was.

It was typical that he should have taken upon himself not only the name of the man who had been known as one of the greatest Rakes in history, but that he had also deliberately emulated his character and his talents.

The Earl of Rochester had been born a Wilmot, and although he was no relation, Wilmot had also been the family name of the man who had made himself a byword for license and rakishness in the Court of Charles II.

It was therefore not entirely surprising that when he was offered an Earldom by King George III, he had asked if he could revive the title of Rochester.

The third Earl of Rochester had died at age eleven. After that the Earldom had become extinct, although the second Earl had never been forgotten.

It had amused the present owner of the title when he was at Eton to read the more bawdy poems of the Restoration Rake and to find a similarity between their two lives.

John Wilmot had had a Puritan mother who blew like a tempest through the lives of her husband, her son, and her son's wife, always disapproving, always railing. His father had been a "thorough good fellow."

Gerald Wilmot could say the same, and it was perhaps a psychological urge to defy his mother and to give her an excuse for her railing which made him continue his research into the life of the man with whom he identified himself.

The Earl of Rochester, in the reign of Charles II, had been a man who, in the words of his Biographer, was a "witty, brave, human, light-hearted débauché."

Perhaps his admirer over a century later would not have been so eager to step into his shoes if his mother had not continually berated him for his boyish excesses and for every prank which could fairly have been attributed to high spirits.

She drove him, the Earl was to think later, into deeper excesses than he had originally contemplated.

Like the Restoration Rochester, he took his seat in the House of Lords at the age of twenty-one, when his father, Lord Wilmot, died. And there was another parallel in his interest in the Navy.

He had passionately denounced the policy by which the Navy was allowed to run down, with the seamen dismissed and put on half-pay, immediately following the signing of the Treaty of Amiens in March 1802.

But before this, the Earl had distinguished himself both by his bravery and by his imagination.

He had brought to safety a great number of the emigrés who were trying to escape from France at the time of the Revolution to save their heads from the guillotine.

As a reward, George III had offered him an Earldom and asked what title he would take. Without hesitation, and with just a faint smile because he knew it would infuriate his mother, Gerald Wilmot had replied:

"The Earl of Rochester—if it pleases Your Majesty!"

He had already earned his nickname.

In his last year at Eton his contemporaries had called him "Rake Wilmot," and the nickname had followed him to Oxford, where it was doubtful if anyone there knew he had any other name.

"Rake Rochester" was exceedingly appropriate and pleased him because once again the comparison was there, bridging the years that lay between the Restoration Rake and the Georgian one which he considered himself to be.

It had been inevitable that he should be a leading light in a gay, raffish circle round the Prince of Wales, and the Queen actually blamed him to some extent for the Prince's licentious behaviour where women were concerned.

If the original Rochester had been a devil with women, then Rake Rochester II was one too.

It was not difficult, because he was not only extremely handsome, tall, and athletic, but he had a Rake's look which combined cynicism with audacity, and a mocking smile with a sadistic tongue.

And of course, as the Restoration Rake wrote satires, the present Earl must do the same, but in prose rather than verse, in speeches rather than in rhyme.

There was only one way in which they differed.

John Rochester had fallen deeply in love and his poems and letters to Elizabeth Barry were as beautiful and as soulful as his other poems were often crude and obscene.

There was no-one in his life now, nor had there ever been, to whom Rake Rochester II could write: *"I do you justice in loving you, so as no woman has ever been loved before."*

Sometimes when he found a woman particularly attractive, the Earl would read the love poems that his predecessor had written to Elizabeth Barry.

> *When with a lover's resistless art,*
> *And her eyes, she did enslave me.*

He told himself he had never felt like that; he had never been enslaved by a woman and he had no wish to be.

Women were there for amusement, for laughter, and for desire, but nothing else.

He had seen only too clearly the hell his mother had made his father's life and he had no intention of suffering in the same way.

He passed from love-affair to love-affair with a swiftness and with at times a ruthlessness which was naturally a subject of comment by the whole of Society.

"Let me make it quite clear," mothers would say protectively to their daughters; "if by some misfortune you are at the same party as Rake Rochester, you will avoid him, and if you disobey me, you will be sent to the country the very next day."

But the sophisticated women with complaisant husbands looked at him with a speculative yearning in their eyes.

The Earl was well aware that he could pick and choose where he pleased, and because it was all too easy he grew particular and more fastidious than he had been in his riotous youth.

Then, after the constrictions and eternal naggings of his boyhood, he had run riot, finding women delectable and making certain of only one thing—that they did not bore him.

That is still an all-important criterion, and he had resisted the blandishments of Lady Langstone for some time.

He was in fact amused and even slightly infatuated with Lady Harriet Sherwood, who had a wild streak in her which made her unpredictable and at times even surprising.

But Lady Langstone, "Circe" as she called herself, was very persistent.

She had chosen her name deliberately, forgetting the banal "Adelaide Charlotte," the names of her Christening, and paraded her power over men, which was quite considerable.

She was in some ways the female counterpart of the Earl, for she took lover after lover, discarding them as soon as they were besotted by her, and looked round for another man to conquer.

She was, the Earl acknowledged, one of the most evilly attractive women he had ever known.

It was not only her haunting, sphinx-like eyes, her dark red hair, and her lips, which could twist enticingly with a promise of unmentionable attractions, but she had a sensuous, feline appearance which made every man who beheld her think of a snake.

"She is the original serpent in the Garden of Eden," a woman had once declared furiously. "It was not a 'he' but a 'she,' and the serpent's name was Circe!"

There were dozens of women who thought the same thing when their husbands had been enticed away from them, when their sons had had their hearts broken and their lives ruined, and when, triumphant and untouched by the havoc she caused, Circe appeared always to be the victor.

There were so many stories about her that the Earl sometimes thought she really was his equal in the Jousts of Love, and if he was not careful he could lose the contest.

Not that he intended to compete with any woman, or any man, for that matter.

The days when he had been young enough to glory in his reputation, to defy his critics by being wilder and even more disreputable than they said he was, were over.

He was still a Rake, but one who could no longer be driven either by his own desires or by other people's.

If he wanted a woman he took her, otherwise he had no intention of showing off to make a Roman Holiday.

Last night, when Circe Langstone had invited him, in just too casual a manner for it to be natural, to visit her this afternoon, he had known exactly what she meant.

"I am entertaining some friends," she had said. "It would be delightful to see you, if you have nothing better to do."

It had been too casual and too artificial for the Earl not to read between the lines and be well aware that at the last moment the friends would be "unavoidably detained" and he would find himself alone with his hostess.

As he looked down at her, with the emeralds round her neck glinting almost as evilly as the green of her eyes, he suddenly felt that after all it might be amusing to find out exactly what she was like, and if she was in fact as bad as she was reputed to be.

A woman's reputation, the Earl well knew, could be built up on a very fragile foundation.

A breath of scandal could be magnified and enlarged upon until a small deviation from the conventional became something which appeared to be more depraved than the depths of hell.

But Circe certainly looked evil, and the Earl knew that the side-long glances under her artificially darkened eye-lashes and the twist of her lips were as artificial as the enigmatic things she said.

Yet there was no doubt that she gave an excellent performance, and he felt that perhaps it would be a mistake not to experience the whole repertoire.

"I am trying out some new horses," he had answered, "and if they please me, as I expect them to do, and I find myself in Park Lane, I might do myself the honour of accepting your invitation."

He spoke with his habitual cynicism, and the look in his eyes told the woman listening that not only would he be quite likely to change his mind at the last moment, but that he was also exceedingly sceptical of being interested if he did call.

Now he was here and the Earl thought that so far everything was exactly as he had expected—with the exception of Ophelia.

The wait in the formal Drawing-Room for the invitation, after he had cooled his heels, to Her Ladyship's *Boudoir,* was all part of the game, which was being played according to a plan.

But Ophelia was certainly a diversion, and even as the door of the *Boudoir* opened, he found himself puzzling as to what had happened to Jem Bullet and why the girl should have said he was not receiving a pension.

* * *

Upstairs, in her small back bedroom, Ophelia asked herself how she could have been so insanely stupid as to have been caught in the Drawing-Room by the Earl of Rochester.

She was well aware how angry her Stepmother would be if she heard of it, and she could only pray that Bateson, the Butler, would be tactful enough not to say that the Earl had found her there still doing the flowers.

There had in fact been more to arrange than usual, which was another reason why she was aware of how important the Earl's visit was.

Ophelia could almost gauge the significance of the men her Stepmother entertained by the amount of flowers that were purchased to augment those that came up every week from the country.

Today, quite an unusually large number of flowers

had been delivered, and after Ophelia had finished in her Stepmother's *Boudoir* there had been no time to complete those in the Drawing-Room.

At the same time, she should have watched the clock, knowing that she should have made herself scarce long before the Earl arrived and was brought upstairs.

"How could I have been so foolish?" she asked herself.

She looked apprehensively in the mirror, seeing not her own reflection but her Stepmother's face, contorted as it was so often with an almost terrifying anger.

Every nerve in Ophelia's body shrank with terror when the woman who had taken her mother's place looked like that.

But she was intelligent enough to be aware that it was not just for the misdeed of the moment that she must suffer, but because she looked like her dead mother and was herself far too attractive for a stepdaughter.

Before she had left School, she had had some idea of what her life would be like. But her anticipations were not half as unpleasant as the reality.

Now, after three months of living with a woman who hated the sight of her, Ophelia wondered frantically how long it could continue.

Nothing she did was right, and she knew that her Stepmother had only to look at her for her eyes to darken and her lips to set in a hard line.

It was no use appealing to her father, because whatever she said, her Stepmother would contradict it, and he would believe his wife.

After two years of marriage he was still infatuated, still completely under the thumb of the woman who had ensnared him almost before his first wife was in her grave.

Ophelia did not know it, but quite a number of people realised that George Langstone had become a widower at exactly the right moment for Circe Drayton.

Her husband, a drunken waster, had at last conveniently got himself killed in a duel, but her lover of the moment had immediately disappeared because he had no wish to marry her.

The men who had been quite content to flatter her, to visit her when her husband was not at home, and even to contribute towards her gowns and jewellery, had no intention of putting what she most desired, which was a second gold band, on her wedding-ring finger.

Without money, with no women-friends, and with a very precarious position in Society, Circe had looked round desperately for someone who would save her, and she had found George Langstone.

He had been easy prey, charming, good-natured, a sportsman, and wealthy, a man who always thought the best both of men and of women.

Circe had turned all her wiles on him and even, some people averred, used Black Magic to get him into her clutches.

Whoever had started the rumour that Circe had invoked the help of Satan may have been activated by spite, but the story had spread like wildfire.

"My dear, she is a witch!" one woman said to another. "And how could Henry, and you know how simple he is, stand up against witchcraft?"

If it was not Henry, it was Leopold or Alexander, Miles, or Lionel.

It certainly seemed as if men were like rabbits mesmerised by a snake, and once they looked into Circe's eyes they were enslaved until she no longer wanted them.

It was in fact Harriet Sherwood more than anyone else who had made the Earl interested in Lady Langstone when he had no intention of following the lead of the herd.

"She is a wicked woman!" Lady Harriet had said violently. "John is in her clutches and I swear it is all due to Black Magic!"

"Can you really believe such nonsense?" the Earl asked.

"But you know John!" Lady Harriet protested. "He is the kindest brother any woman ever had. He is quiet

and sensible, and has never before cared for anyone
but his wife and family."

"Then perhaps it is time he sowed a few wild oats!"
the Earl remarked cynically.

"Wild oats? At thirty-four?" Lady Harriet retorted.
"He should have been past all that nonsense a long time
ago! But it is not his fault. I do not blame him. It is
that woman, that wicked, evil witch! He did not have
a chance of escaping her."

She had been so upset about her brother and so
violent in her denunciation of Circe Langstone and her
Black Magic that the Earl had found himself mildly
curious.

He was well aware of the invitation in Lady Langstone's eyes when she looked at him. He also knew,
from the way she sometimes pointedly ignored him, that
it was a challenge which most men found irresistible.

But he merely watched her with half-closed eyes and
a mocking smile which told her that, if nothing else, her
performance did not deceive him.

Now, finally, he was succumbing. But not too far,
he told himself.

Only a little reconnoitring to see if she was as false
as he suspected her to be and if her vaunted powers of
seduction had merely been magnified by those who
hated her.

To Ophelia he was just another in the long train of
her Stepmother's lovers, which made her feel sick and
disgusted because she saw how blatantly her Stepmother was deceiving her father.

It offended everything she believed in as sacred to
think that this woman should have taken her mother's
place, this woman who was now sleeping in her mother's
bed and wearing her mother's jewels.

If Circe hated her stepdaughter, Ophelia despised
anyone who had sunk so low and who could be so
deceitful.

But she was also physically afraid, and that was
something she had never been before.

She wondered now, with apprehension that was almost a pain, if, despite what she had said, the Earl

would tell her Stepmother that she had spoken to him of Jem Bullet.

She wondered how she had been brave enough, and yet she felt despairingly that she must help the poor man, who was living on the verge of starvation.

It was his daughter who, when she was maiding Ophelia, had told her of the penury to which he had been reduced.

"You'd think a gentleman like the Earl of Rochester, Miss," Emily had said, "would've more consideration than to let me poor father die o' starvation, after all th' years he'd served him."

"Surely the Earl gave him a pension when he had to leave his service?"

"Not a penny, Miss," Emily said, shaking her head.

"Why did your father not get in touch with the Earl?"

"He couldn't walk at first after the accident, Miss," Emily replied, "and when he could move about with a stick, he goes down to Rochester Castle and sees His Lordship's Agent."

"What did he say?" Ophelia asked.

"He told him he'd do what he could, but his Master were close-fisted to those as were no longer any use t' him."

"It is disgraceful!" Ophelia exclaimed. "I cannot imagine Papa behaving like that towards anyone who had worked for us."

Even as she spoke, she knew that if her father would not do so her Stepmother would, and she supposed that Society people were not like her mother, for they could never see anyone suffering without trying to help them.

Because Emily had made her feel so sorry for Jem Bullet, she had insisted on going to see him.

She and Emily had driven in a hackney-carriage because Lady Langstone would never have allowed her stepdaughter to use her own carriage, and Ophelia was appalled at the slums through which they passed round Lambeth.

When finally they reached the house in which Jem Bullet was living, she had hardly believed that a human being could be condemned to exist in a place in which no reputable farmer would have housed his pigs.

The floor was clean—Jem had seen to that—but the walls were running with damp, the doors had rusted on their hinges, and the glass had long since been knocked out of the windows.

Ophelia had very little money of her own, in fact only just enough to pay for a few simple gowns and any small things she required.

Even that was resented by her Stepmother, who always spoke as if Ophelia were too wealthy to need any assistance from her father, and she resented even the food which they put in Ophelia's mouth, because she said they could not afford it.

This of course was nonsense, as Ophelia's father was a rich man. When his first wife had been alive, he had showered presents on her and she could buy anything she required for herself and Ophelia.

Ophelia left Jem as much money as she had with her, even though he protested at her generosity. She also promised that when her quarterly allowance came due, she would give Emily some more for him.

She considered asking her father if he would help Jem. But once, when she had asked for some money with which to buy herself a new gown because those she wore were outgrown and shabby, her Stepmother had made such a scene that she decided, proudly, that she would never beg again.

Ever since she had visited Jem in Lambeth she had hated the Earl as she hated few other people.

Of course she had heard of him.

Even the girls at School had repeated stories that they had heard from their mothers and had warned one another that they must never, by any mischance, be seen in his company.

"Mama says he is the Devil himself!" one girl had said. "But quite frankly, he is so very handsome that I should rather like to meet him."

"And if you do, you will not be asked to any of the Balls!" another girl warned. "Mama told me how the daughter of one lady whom the Earl fancied was ostracised completely."

"That is not fair!" Ophelia exclaimed. "She could not help what her mother was doing!"

"Mama says you cannot touch pitch without being defiled!" was the answer.

Ophelia supposed that that was true. At the same time, knowing how much the Earl spent on his horses, it seemed incredible that he should be so mean to a man who had been unable to continue in his employment through no fault of his own.

Jem had told her how it had happened.

He was taking a very spirited horse over a high jump that the Earl had had erected in his Park.

"I'd have got him over it ordinarily, Miss," the old jockey said, "but a bird upsets him; flying out of th' hedge just as he jumped! Down he goes, and rolls over on top o' me."

"Oh, I am sorry!" Ophelia said.

"He were a good horse, and I liked riding him. He'd not have done it on purpose. 'Twas just a bit o' bad luck."

Ophelia was touched that the man did not blame the horse, but when she drove home with Emily she had certainly blamed the Earl for his callousness and what amounted almost to cruelty.

She had in fact never expected to see him face-to-face.

Her Stepmother was entertaining several other men, none of whom merited an extensive amount of extra flowers.

When unexpectedly early this morning Ophelia had been sent for, she had gone apprehensively into her Stepmother's bedroom, wondering what she had done wrong.

To her surprise, she found Circe sitting up in bed and in a remarkably good humour.

Although it was agony to see her as she had seen her mother so often in the morning, Ophelia had to admit that her Stepmother looked extremely attractive.

Her long red hair, which reached nearly to her waist, was hanging over her shoulders.

She had not yet applied the numerous cosmetics

which stood in bottles and pots in great profusion on
her dressing-table.

Yet her skin was very white and clear, and her eyes,
even with no mascara on her eye-lashes, were green
and at the same time mysterious.

"I have sent out for some flowers, Ophelia," Lady
Langstone said, "and kindly do them a little better than
you did them last week."

Ophelia did not reply.

She knew quite well that the flowers had been well
done, because her mother had taught her how to arrange
them, but her Stepmother could never say anything
pleasant.

"I want lilies, freesias, and tuberoses in the *Boudoir*,"
she said. "Fill the fireplace, as it is too hot for a fire,
and see that vases are standing on every table, especially round the couch."

"I will do that, Stepmama," Ophelia replied.

"So I should hope!" Circe Langstone said with a hard
note in her voice. "You do little enough, and if you
are not useful, what is the point of keeping a tiresome
girl in the house?"

Ophelia did not reply, and her Stepmother went on:

"The rest of the flowers are to go in the Drawing-
Room, and try to use some imagination. I could actually
see the back of the grate the last time you attempted to
fill the fireplace!"

"There were ... not enough flowers," Ophelia murmured.

"Excuses! Always excuses!" Lady Langstone ejacu-
lated in a sudden rage. "For God's sake, get out of my
sight! It makes me tired to look at you!"

It did not make her tired, Ophelia thought as she went
from the bedroom; it made her jealous.

She had known as soon as Circe Drayton married
her father that despite the fact that she had caught him
and was now his wife, she was jealous of the woman to
whom he had been so happily married for eighteen
years.

She tried to disparage everything that belonged to
the first Lady Langstone—not in her husband's hearing,
of course, for she was too clever for that.

But her spiteful remarks, her jeering laughter, and her unceasing unpleasantness about the woman whose place she had taken made Ophelia clench her hands and have to exert an almost superhuman self-control not to answer back.

At first she had been stupid enough to do so, where-upon her Stepmother had not only slapped her face but had even beaten her with one of her husband's riding-whips.

She had also complained to her husband that his daughter was rude.

"Of course, darling, I understand it," she had said. "All little girls are jealous of their fathers, but her antagonism makes me unhappy, and I know you do not want that."

Lord Langstone had taken his daughter to task.

"I know you miss your mother, Ophelia," he said, "and so do I, but Circe is now my wife and you must treat her with proper respect."

"I try to . . . Papa."

"Then try a little harder," her father said. "I want Circe to be happy. She tells me you have been very obstinate and quite unnecessarily rude."

It was impossible to tell her father that she had merely been defending the memory of her mother, whom they had both loved.

Ophelia had learnt quickly to keep her feelings to herself and to bite back the words that trembled on her lips.

But it was agony to listen to the disparaging things that were said deliberately, merely to hurt her.

"Who could have chosen such a ridiculous colour for these curtains?" Lady Langstone would ask. "Such vulgar taste, if you can call it taste at all!"

She had relegated a fine portrait of her predecessor not to the attic—Ophelia would have understood that—but to the Servants' Hall.

"It is just the right place for it," she said. "I am sure the servants will enjoy having her there."

At night Ophelia would cry bitterly and plan that she would run away and ask one of her mother's cousins if she could live with them.

But she knew it would hurt her father to feel that she did not wish to live with him, and she had the uncomfortable feeling that, just to punish her, her Stepmother would deliberately bring her back.

She was beginning to have her uses in the house: there were the flowers to be arranged, clothes to be mended, and Library books to be exchanged.

Not that her Stepmother read very much. She only kept up with what the current topic was at the moment —Lord Byron's poems, and Sir Walter Scott's latest novel.

A few quick glances, then Ophelia had to take them back again—but not before she had read them herself!

Even though she was sometimes kept busy, there were long hours when she had nothing to do except read.

Her Stepmother had made it very clear that she had no wish for her to meet her friends or for it to be known that she was even in the house.

"I am too young to chaperone a young girl," she said firmly, "and so no-one is to realise that you are living with your father and me. Is that clear?"

"Yes . . . Stepmama."

"If I find you forcing yourself on people who call here, I shall be extremely annoyed! What is more, you certainly will not do it again!"

There was no doubt of the menace in her Stepmother's voice, and Ophelia said quickly:

"I will not let . . . anyone see . . . me."

When her father and Stepmother were alone, which was very seldom, she dined with them, and she supposed that her father never noticed that when they entertained she did not appear.

Anyway he said nothing, and Ophelia sometimes felt as if she were a ghost moving about the house when it was quiet and silent, and hiding in her bedroom when there was laughter and the chatter of voices in the Drawing-Room.

She walked to the window now and stood looking out.

"How could I have been so stupid as to let the Earl find me in the Drawing-Room?" she asked herself again, and thought how angry her Stepmother would be if she heard of it.

She felt a shiver run through her, and saw that her hands, lying on the window-ledge, were trembling.

Chapter Two

If the Earl was intelligent, so was Circe Langstone.

He was well aware what he could expect to find when he called on her in the afternoon when her husband would be gambling at his Club.

However, when the Earl entered the *Boudoir* where, to him there was the very familiar scent of tuberoses and lilies, he found his hostess not, as he had expected, lying on a chaise-longue, but writing at her *secrétaire*.

She had her back to him and glanced over her shoulder to say:

"Forgive me, My Lord, but I have an urgent letter to finish. I think you will find something to amuse you on the stool in front of the fireplace."

Before the Earl could reply, Lady Langstone added to the Butler:

"Wait, Bateson. I have a letter to be carried immediately to the Duchess of Devonshire. As it is urgent, send one of the grooms with it."

"Very good, M'Lady," Bateson said, waiting at the open door.

The Earl, with an amused twinkle in his eyes, walked, as he had been asked to do, towards the long, tapestry-covered stool which stood in front of the fireplace.

There the scent of the flowers was rather overwhelming, but he noticed that they had been arranged with an elegance which he thought was obviously due to Ophelia.

She had, he was certain, an artistic sense to complement her appearance.

Lady Langstone went on writing and he picked up the book from the stool and saw that it was a volume of Restoration Poems, illustrated with wood-cuts that at first glance told him what to expect.

The poems were lewd and obscene and lacking the genius which had characterised those written by Lord Rochester, and they were coarse in a manner which would have disgusted any ordinary woman.

Lady Langstone rose from her *secrétaire* and walked across the room to hand the letter to the waiting Butler.

As she did so, the Earl thought with amusement that she was determined to be different from what he might have expected.

He had in fact anticipated that not only would she be lying on the chaise-longue, but dressed in a diaphanous negligé such as were always worn by the women who expected him to make love to them.

But, unexpectedly, Circe Langstone was wearing a gown that on anyone else would have looked staid and even respectable.

But although it was made of quite thick material and was not transparent, as was the fashion, it clung to her sensuous body, and once again the Earl was reminded of a snake, which he remembered shed its skin at regular intervals.

The Butler took the note and left the room, and as the door closed behind him, Lady Langstone said:

"Bess Devonshire was to have been here this afternoon to meet you, but unfortunately she has contracted a chill and must therefore keep to her bed."

The Earl did not believe a word of this but he had to admit that the explanation was skilfully performed, and he watched Circe Langstone a little more appreciatively as she settled herself in an arm-chair.

It was on the other side of the fireplace, where it would have been impossible, even if he had wished to, to sit near her.

"What do you think of the book I found for you?" she asked.

"It was kind of you to take the trouble."

"It was not really much trouble," she answered. "I saw it in George's Library some months ago, and only when you were coming here this afternoon did I remember that it might amuse you."

The Earl seated himself in a chair opposite her, with the width of the hearth-rug between them.

"Does this sort of thing interest you?" he asked, putting the book down on the stool as he spoke.

"It depends on with whom one reads it!" Circe Langstone replied, and now there was undoubtedly a note in her voice which the Earl had been expecting.

* * *

It was after Ophelia had left her Stepmother's bedroom that Circe had lain back against the lace-edged pillows to plan her campaign.

She had for a long time been determined to get the Earl of Rochester into her clutches, but she knew that he was aware of it and that for the moment he was on his guard.

Like all demanding women, Circe always wanted what was not hers.

Although since her marriage there had been innumerable men prepared to beg her favours, she had found their conquest all too easy and therefore she was always looking over their shoulders for somebody else.

Since she had married Lord Langstone so easily and with what she knew was only a minimum of effort on her part, she had begun to think herself infallible.

It was true that few men at whom she had looked with a special light in her eyes and an invitation on her lips had had the strength to refuse her.

At the same time, she told herself that most of them were not worth the taking, and though for a short while they assuaged her greed for passionate sensation, invariably she would be back in the field looking for another prey.

The Earl of Rochester was the most elusive, distinguished, best-looking man in the *Beau Monde*.

To Circe Langstone his reputation only added to his attractions, and she found herself feeling a flicker of excitement at the thought of what they could mean to each other once he desired her as she desired him.

She took a great deal of trouble to find out everything she could about him, but it was not as easy as it sounded.

Nearly all the women with whom he had been enamoured had, in fact, sooner or later fallen in love with him, and strangely they would not talk about him or the part he had played in their lives.

Even those he had discarded ruthlessly were silent because they would not admit that they had failed to hold him, and anyway Circe Langstone was not the type of woman in whom another woman would confide.

She began to think that his reputation was not as bad as it had been made out to be, and yet with his raffish appearance and above all the commotion which his satirical speeches caused in the House of Lords, his reputation was not without foundation.

Those he berated with his sarcastic tongue, and there were few Ministers who escaped his attention, would sit glowering with crimson faces, Circe learnt, as he verbally flayed them to the point where even their most ardent supporters turned against them.

She learnt that when the Earl walked into the Chamber, which fortunately was not too often, there was a hush of apprehension and the Ministers concerned with the subjects in which he was interested passed their tongues over their dry lips.

It was, although Circe did not realise it, another echo from the Restoration, when the King's mistresses, each powerful in her own sphere, had cause to be uneasy.

Age was their implacable and incorruptible enemy, and they found their wrinkles, their thinning hair, and their decaying teeth recorded in Rochester's merciless poetry.

Circe was not the least interested in Rake Rochester's public utterances.

What she wanted to learn was the intimate details of his private life. Was he as good a lover as he was reputed to be? Was his nickname a true indication of his character?

When the Earl had accepted her invitation yesterday, she had known a feeling of elation that she had not experienced for some time.

At last he had risen to the bait she had thrown at him so skilfully, but without any apparent success, for the last six months.

As always, when she wanted something, a man or a jewel, Circe concentrated her mind and found it difficult to think of anything else.

There were no lengths to which she would not go to gain her own ends. There were no methods she would not stoop to use.

This had included visiting a very dubious part of London and being ensconced inside a dingy, unpleasant house in a sordid back-street.

Now, she told herself as she looked at the Earl, every effort had been worthwhile.

She bent forward to pick up the book which he had thrown back onto the stool, which stood between them.

"There is a picture here which might amuse you," she said.

She turned over the pages with her long fingers and the Earl saw that once again, contrary to his expectations, she wore no jewellery except for one enormous emerald ring on her left hand.

She looked up at him, her eyes beneath her dark lashes as green as the emerald on her finger.

"This might make you look," she said, "unless of course you are easily shocked?"

The Earl knew that he was expected to rise and go to her side to sit on the arm of her chair, where doubtless the perfume she wore would be as exotic as the tuberoses.

"I am more interested in learning about you at the moment," he said without moving. "Tell me about yourself. You have a reputation, My Lady, and that is not surprising."

"Why is it not surprising?" Circe enquired.

"Because beautiful women invariably evoke the jealousy of their contemporaries."

"So you think I am beautiful?"

"If I thought otherwise I would hardly have been so impolite as to say so."

"In which case I shall answer your compliment by paying you one myself. Your reputation, My Lord, is even worse than mine."

"It depends by whose standards we judge ourselves," the Earl remarked. "A reputation can often be a subtle deception for those who believe all they hear."

Circe Langstone leant back in her chair.

"I have been curious about you, My Lord," she said, "simply because although so many people denounce you violently, their accusations seldom go into details."

"And that would interest you?" the Earl flashed.

"But of course! If we are calculating our points one by one, we obviously have to be a little better informed than our attackers."

The Earl was amused.

This was a different approach from that which women usually made in his direction.

He was well aware that the trap was set and he only had to take one short step to be caught in it.

He wondered if he should do so, when suddenly, quite involuntarily, he saw in his mind the expression of terror in Ophelia's face when he had entered the Drawing-Room.

In all his dealings with women, with all the recriminations, the tears, the appeals, and the pleas to which he had listened over the years, he was certain that he had never evoked in a woman the terror that he had seen in Ophelia's eyes.

"Please ... please do not tell ... Stepmother that I have ... spoken to ... you of Jem Bullet."

He could hear the sheer, undiluted fear behind the whispered words.

He felt suddenly that the woman sitting opposite him had lost the sensuous attraction of which he had been conscious ever since he had entered the room.

She was not a woman but a serpent, the reptile that was loathed by every white man.

He could remember, when he had been in India, his dislike of the snake-charmers and the insistence with

which he had always ordered his servants to search his
bedroom before he retired to rest.

Instead of Circe in her green gown sitting opposite
him, he saw a cobra spreading its hood, its forked
tongue flashing in and out, its whole body swaying
slightly as it prepared to strike.

Slowly, languidly, he rose to his feet.

"I have enjoyed our conversation, Lady Langstone,"
he said, "but my horses are still fresh, and I must not
keep them waiting. Perhaps I may have the pleasure
of calling on you another afternoon?"

He saw a sudden streak of lightning in Circe's eyes
before she replied quietly:

"But of course, My Lord, I understand. Horses, unlike women, always come first in a man's estima-
tion."

She rose from her chair and walked ahead of him to
the door.

As she reached it, she turned and held out the hand
with the emerald ring.

He raised it to his lips, but his mouth did not actually touch her skin.

Just for a moment her fingers tightened on his, with
an almost indiscernible pressure, then the door was
opened and she walked with him to the top of the
staircase.

She watched him walk down towards the Hall, but
when he had taken his hat from the attendant flunkey,
he glanced back and saw that she was no longer there.

* * *

Lady Langstone moved back to her *Boudoir,* an
expression on her face which would have made her
stepdaughter pale.

What had happened? Why had he left her so quickly?

She had been so certain in her own mind that by the
end of the afternoon she would be in his arms and
would have aroused in him the wild, uncontrollable
desire that most men experienced when she looked at
them from under her eye-lashes and moved her lips
invitingly.

She thought she knew every step of the game, every

provocative word and gesture which had never failed in the past to make a man bemused, intrigued, and finally infatuated.

But somehow, even when she thought she had the Earl in the net, he had slipped out and eluded her.

How was it possible? How could it have happened to her when she had been so sure that what she had desired for so long was finally in her grasp?

She walked about the room, backwards and forwards, beset by her thoughts, conscious of an exasperation and an irritation which at the same time was subservient to her need always to get her own way.

"I will have him! He will be mine!" she told herself with a positiveness that she felt in the past had sent out to her victims powerful rays which they were unable to ignore.

She felt that she had a power within herself, a force that could strike like an arrow into the most vital and receptive part of a man, so that for him there was no escape.

The explanation must be either that the Earl's critics had exaggerated and he could not live up to his name, or else that he was determined not to capitulate as easily as she had hoped and expected.

Lady Langstone stood still, closing her eyes and clasping her hands together.

Then she formed a mental picture of the Earl driving away from her house, and her thoughts followed him relentlessly, her whole being holding him despite his desire to escape.

"Come to me! Come to me!"

Every nerve in her body was intensified in the fire she felt pouring out from her towards him, following him, invading him, seeping into his mind.

She concentrated to the point where she felt almost exhausted, then threw herself down on the chaise-longue with its satin cushions, and, putting her hand to her lips, she let her tongue flicker over the huge emerald.

The door of her Sitting-Room opened and her maid came in.

Marie was her one confidante, the one person in

the world before whom she enacted no theatricals, made no pretences.

"I hear Milor leave!" Marie stated.

After twenty years in London she still had a strong French accent.

"Yes, he left," Circe said sulkily. "Where did I go wrong? Why did he go?"

" 'E weel come back," Marie said soothingly. "Eff you do as Zenobe say."

"She says a lot of things that do not come true," Circe Langstone replied, "and as for that Priest—I do not believe in him."

"Non, non, Milady! You wrong, sometimes theengs do not work out as you expec'. You must wait. You must 'ave ze patience."

"Patience!" Lady Langstone said. "That is something I do not have! I want him! And I intend to have him!"

Marie picked up a Chinese shawl embroidered in exquisite colours and put it over her mistress's knees.

"Hélas!" Marie said. "Let Milor depar'. 'E weel come back. 'E weel not escape."

'I must ask Zenobe what went wrong,' Lady Langstone thought to herself.

"It might 'ave been to do with . . . *non* . . . *c'est impossible!"*

"What is impossible?"

"Eet might be sometheeng Mees Ophelia said to heem."

"Miss Ophelia?"

Lady Langstone's voice rang out like a pistol-shot.

"What do you mean by that?"

"She was een the Drawing-Room when Milor arrive."

"In the Drawing-Room," Lady Langstone repeated in a low voice.

She threw back the shawl with which Marie had covered her legs and rose from the chaise-longue.

"Non, non, Milady. Do not agitate yourself," Marie begged. "I should not 'ave told you, but I think in my mind eet is unfortunate."

"I have told her to keep out of sight," Lady Langstone said furiously. "I will not have her meeting any of my friends, least of all the Earl of Rochester."

She crossed the room and pulled open the drawer of a beautiful inlaid French commode.

She took from it a thin leather whip. Then, leaving the room, she slammed the door behind her.

Marie picked up the shawl and folded it, shaking her head as if at her own thoughts, but her thin lips were smiling.

*   *   *

The Earl arrived at Rochester Castle the following morning.

He had not notified his servants of his coming, but in all his houses he expected his staff to be ready at any time he chose to visit.

Rochester Castle, because it was near to London and he kept a great number of his horses there, was in fact always prepared for His Lordship to appear, and as likely as not to bring a large party of friends with him.

He drove his Chef, who was very temperamental, nearly to madness, as he never knew how many he would have to cater for and he might be given only a few short hours in which to prepare a dinner-party for twenty or thirty persons.

As he drove down the drive, the Earl thought that the Castle always looked its best at this time of year.

The lilacs, purple and white, were in bloom, the laburnum were hung with chains of gold, and the kingcups bordered the lake on which moved the swans which had been at the Castle for the last fifty years.

There was no flag flying from the heights of the tower, but the Earl knew that immediately on his arrival the servants would run it up to flutter in the breeze.

He asked himself, as he had done before, why he spent so much time in London when the country could be more alluring than any woman.

The man he emulated had retired to the country

every year, to write, to recover from sickness, or for contemplation.

The Earl recalled two of his lines:

When to your banks and bowers I came distressed
Half dead through absence, seeking peace and rest . . .

He then smiled, reflecting that he was certainly not "half dead," for, unlike his predecessor, he did not drink to excess!

So where he was concerned he did not have to limit his "fancy for wine and fancy for women."

For a moment he thought of Lady Harriet and what her anger would be like if he became interested in Circe!

Then, bored with the idea of a scene, he remembered that he had bought a pair of horses at Tattersall's early in the week. By now they would have arrived at his stables and he looked forward to driving them.

But he was determined first to find out about Jem Bullet.

He did not know why, but the girl's accusation that he had not pensioned off a valued servant was an irritation from which he could not escape.

Last night, when he had retired to bed in the early hours after dining with a number of special friends, he found himself thinking not of the manner in which they had beguiled themselves when dinner was over with some of the prettiest Cyprians in London, but of Ophelia's pleading words and the look of condemnation in her eyes.

"Damn the girl! Why can she not get her facts right?" he had asked himself.

Yet it had irritated him to the point where he decided that first thing in the morning, when he was called, he would go to the Castle and find for himself the proof that she was wrong.

The Earl was in fact generous not only to the women he seduced and to those who contributed to his amusement, but also to those who served him.

He was not a spendthrift by any means, but as he

did not stint himself, neither did he stint those round him.

Besides, he had always believed that most servants were worthy of his hire, and if those who served him were content, they were less likely to be disloyal or dishonest.

"Will Your Lordship be returning to London this evening?" Jason asked now.

"No, I shall stay the night," the Earl replied.

As he spoke, he pulled up outside the front door with its long wide steps that were part of the magnificent alterations to the house which had been effected by the Earl's grandfather.

Then the Castle had been Wilmot Castle, and the Earl had deliberately changed the name to annoy both his mother and his other relations who criticised him.

"It has always been Wilmot Castle," one of his cousins had expostulated, "and Wilmots have lived there for the last three hundred years."

"A Rochester is living there now!" the Earl had replied defiantly.

His childhood had been unhappy at the Castle because of the manner in which his mother treated him.

Yet, since he inherited, he fondly believed it to be a happy place not only for himself and his friends, but also for the people who lived and worked there.

In the past he had given many riotous parties that might almost have been termed "orgies," but now in what he termed his "wiser years" he preferred to entertain more intimately, which usually meant his favourite of the moment.

When he was not entertaining or being entertained, he devoted his time to his horses.

Somebody must have spotted the Phaeton coming down the drive, for by the time the Earl had climbed the steps, the door was opened and there was quite a pleasing array of footmen in their spectacular livery of purple and gold, with his Major-Domo bowing a welcome.

"Your Lordship's other guests will be arriving later?" the Major-Domo enquired.

"There are no other guests, Poulson," the Earl replied. "I will have a drink, then visit the stables."

"Very good, M'Lord."

A bottle of champagne at exactly the right temperature was being offered him within a few minutes of his having entered the Library, where he habitually sat.

"Will Your Lordship require something to eat?" the Major-Domo asked.

"No, I had luncheon on the way," the Earl replied.

He sipped the champagne appreciatively, thinking it was better than what the Prince of Wales had served at Carlton House when he had dined there two evenings ago.

Then, as his Major-Domo was leaving the room, he asked:

"Is Aslett in the Estate Office?"

"I'm afraid not, M'Lord. He wasn't expecting Your Lordship, but he's somewhere in the grounds. I saw him ride out of the stables about half-an-hour ago."

"Tell him I want to see him when he returns."

"Very good, M'Lord. Shall I send a groom to look for him?"

The Earl hesitated, then replied:

"There is no hurry."

He put down his glass of champagne and walked down the long passages to the West Wing of the house, where the Estate Office had been recently installed.

In his father's day it had been situated in the house in which the Agent himself lived.

But it meant a special journey every time the Earl wished to look at a map, the pedigrees of his horses, or anything else in which he was personally interested.

He therefore had had a large room, on the ground floor of the Castle, specially furnished with files, bookcases, and maps, so that everything was at his hand anytime he wished to see it.

He reached the door of the Office and walked in, expecting to find working there an elderly woman who helped the Agent with the correspondence.

The room was empty and, as he appreciated, very tidy.

He knew what he required, and that was a large ledger in which was noted all those who had been pensioned off in his father's time and been added to in his own.

He opened quite a number of drawers before finally he found it. Then he sat down in a chair at the desk.

Now he would prove Ophelia Langstone wrong and she could apologise to him for making such a fundamental mistake.

He opened the ledger.

The names were in alphabetical order and he saw that there were quite a number in the *A* group.

One or two of the early pensioners had been crossed out and the word "dead" written over them.

There still seemed to be a sizeable list, however, and the Earl turned over the page to the *B*s.

He had been right.

Jem Bullet was listed, and what was more, his pension had been increased twice since he had been retired. Now he was receiving monthly a sum which would certainly keep him in the necessities of life and provide quite a number of comforts as well.

"I wonder who could have told Miss Langstone such a lie?" he asked himself.

Then beneath Jem's name he saw written "Walter Bullingham."

Walter Bullingham!

The Earl remembered him well: he had been an old man when the Earl had inherited.

He looked at the name and looked again.

Strange—he could have sworn that Walter Bullingham was dead. He seemed to remember telling somebody to send a wreath to the funeral. But it was obvious that he was mistaken, because Bullingham had been receiving his pension every month and had, like Bullet, had it raised.

He now turned over the pages of the ledger one by one.

It was amazing how healthy all his pensioners were! In the *C*s, *D*s, *E*s, and *F*s, apparently no-one had died in the last ten years!

Then he saw a name he knew very well: Graham—Nanny Graham.

He certainly remembered her, and she was alive, as he had expected her to be.

He could remember when she had retired and gone to live with her old mother, who had once been Housekeeper at the Castle. A frightening old woman!

He remembered being very much in awe of her when he was a boy, when she had moved about the Castle in her black dress with her chatelaine clanking at her side.

He particularly disliked her because she would tell his mother if any of his misdeeds concerned her part of the Castle.

She must be very old by now. Astonishingly, she too was alive!

The Earl stared at the ledger incredulously. Then he rose from the desk and, carrying the book under his arm, left the room.

When he reached the Hall he said to a footman:

"Run to the stables and ask to have my Chaise sent round immediately with two horses—the new chestnuts."

"Very good, M'Lord."

The Earl walked into the Library and waited impatiently.

Then, as a thought struck him, he put the ledger away in a drawer of his large desk and locked it.

Because he was impatient it seemed a long time before a footman announced that the Chaise was waiting for him.

He stepped into it and picked up the reins, and the frown that was between his eyes lightened a little when he saw the new chestnuts, for he thought they looked even better than they had in the Sale-Room.

It was not Jason who sat beside him but Bert, one of the young grooms under old Winchbold, who had been at the Castle for over thirty years.

"They are good horse-flesh, Bert," the Earl said when they were halfway down the drive.

"Best I've seen, M'Lord, an' a perfect pair. Not a hair's difference between 'em!"

The Earl liked the enthusiasm in the young groom's voice, and they talked of the other horses in his stables until they reached the village.

The length of the drive took them nearly three miles from the Castle, but the village was on the Earl's Estate and there was a long line of black and white thatched cottages, which, standing in their small gardens, had been built by his father just before he died.

As the Earl reached them, he pulled in his horses.

"I have forgotten, Bert," he said, "at which house does Nanny Graham live?"

"Last but one from the end, M'Lord," Bert said, "and it's excited she'll be to see Your Lordship!"

The Earl was certain that this was true and thought it must be four or five years since he had last seen his old Nurse.

His Comptroller had always reminded Aslett which people should be specially remembered at Christmas, and the Earl was certain that Nanny Graham would not think he had forgotten her.

He stepped from the Chaise and opened the small wooden gate.

He saw that the garden was exactly as he might have expected it, with primroses, daffodils, and tulips, and with a clump of narcissus on either side of the front door.

Nanny had always loved flowers, he remembered, and had insisted on having them in the Nursery, much to his mother's annoyance.

"It makes the place cheerful, M'Lady," he now remembered Nanny saying, when as usual his mother was finding fault with everything that concerned him.

He knocked on the door and a voice said:
"Come in!"

He walked in to find Nanny Graham standing at the table, in a white apron, just as he remembered her, stirring something in a bowl.

She looked up to see him, large and broad-shouldered and seeming to fill the whole tiny kitchen, and she gave an exclamation as she put down her bowl and wooden spoon.

"Master Gerald!" she exclaimed. "Here—and me not expecting you!"

The Earl thought it was a long time since anyone had called him by his real name.

"I only arrived at the Castle an hour ago, Nanny," he said. "But I wanted to see you."

"See me, Master Gerald?" Nanny asked.

She wiped her hands on a cloth which the Earl saw was spotlessly clean, as was the apron with which she covered her grey dress.

"Yes," the Earl replied. "I want you to tell me certain things."

"Then come into the Parlour, M'Lord."

"I am quite happy to sit here," the Earl replied with a twinkle in his eyes, "and if that is a cake you are baking, I would like a piece of it."

"A cake!" Nanny exclaimed. "I haven't been able to make one for a year or more. That's bread I'm mixing, and . . ."

She checked what she was about to say, and instead added:

"We'll sit in the Parlour, as is proper. The kitchen's not the place for you, M'Lord."

The Earl thought it was pointless to argue, and therefore, bending his head because the doorway was so low, he went from the kitchen across the very small passage and into the tiny Parlour on the other side of it.

There was only just room for a horse-hair sofa, a small arm-chair, and a round table on which, as he would have expected, stood a vase filled with daffodils beside a Bible.

He looked at the Bible and thought that, like his mother's railing, this was one of the things he had most hated when he was a child.

When he was naughty Nanny would make him copy out as many lines from the Bible as fitted the punishment.

Because he knew it was expected of him, the Earl sat down on the sofa, and Nanny, having removed her apron, stood with her hands folded, waiting.

"Sit down, Nanny," the Earl commanded. "As I have said—I want to talk to you. Are you pleased to see me?"

"You look well enough, M'Lord," Nanny replied, "but I daresay all those late nights take their toll of even the strongest constitution."

"Late nights?" the Earl enquired. "And what do you know about them?"

"What I hears, Master Gerald, and it's not always what I would wish," Nanny answered repressively.

The Earl laughed.

"I have not come to talk about myself or my health, but about your mother."

"My mother, M'Lord?"

"She is alive?"

Nanny smiled.

"If she was, she'd be a hundred and two come this next July, and there's not many people as reaches that age."

"When did she die?"

"Nine years ago come next Michaelmas, and although I shouldn't say it, it was a merciful release from her suffering."

"I thought she must be dead," the Earl mused. "And you, Nanny? You are getting your pension regularly?"

There was a little pause.

"Yes . . . M'Lord."

There was something in the way Nanny spoke which made the Earl look at her sharply.

"What is wrong?" he asked.

"I didn't say as anything was wrong, Master Gerald," Nanny replied in a defensive tone which the Earl had heard many years ago when she spoke to his mother.

"If there is nothing wrong, then something is not right," the Earl insisted. "Tell me the truth, Nanny. After all these years we should be able to speak frankly to each other."

"That's true, Master Gerald, but I don't like to complain."

"But that is exactly what I want you to do," the

Earl said. "I have a feeling things are wrong and I want you to help me to put them right."

Nanny Graham looked at him to see if he was serious, then she said:

"Well, since you asks me, M'Lord, things have grown expensive since the war, and a penny and a shilling don't go so far as they used to do."

"Will you tell me exactly what you are receiving every week?" the Earl asked.

"What I've always had, M'Lord, and all the others in the village too. I manage because I does a little sewing for the Vicar's wife, but for some it's almost impossible to make ends meet."

The Earl's lips tightened, then he said:

"There has been a mistake, Nanny, but it will not occur again in the future. Both you and everyone else who is pensioned will have the money they have been receiving trebled, with back payments for a year in a lump sum."

For a moment Nanny Graham sat very still, and the Earl liked her control over her feelings, which he remembered. Then she said in a voice that shook a little:

"You really—mean that, M'Lord?"

"I mean it," the Earl said, "and I can only apologise for my negligence in allowing myself and all of you to be defrauded for so long."

Nanny looked at him and he said:

"Defrauded is the right word. Do you know of anybody else who has been suffering as you have been?"

"I don't like to point suspicion where it might be unfounded, M'Lord," Nanny said, "but if I was you I'd have a talk with some of Your Lordship's tenant-farmers. I've heard they're dissatisfied, but it's for them to speak for themselves."

"Thank you, Nanny."

The Earl rose to his feet and she rose too, saying:

"You'll take care of yourself, Master Gerald? And it's time you were getting married. I've no wish to die until I've held your son in my arms."

"I am afraid that in that case, Nanny, you will have to wait until you are at least a hundred and two, or over!" the Earl said.

He saw the expression on his Nurse's face and put his hand on her shoulder.

"I am happy as I am, Nanny, make no mistake about that, and I have no wish to be 'leg-shackled' as they used to say in the village when someone got married."

He thought of quoting John Rochester's bitter words on matrimony, which he often repeated to himself:

> Of all the Bedlams marriage is the worst,
> With endless cords, with endless keepers curst!
> Frantic with love you run, and rave about,
> Mad to get in, but hopeless to get out.

The words were on the Earl's lips then, but he knew they would shock Nanny and he repressed them.

"You'll find a nice young lady one of these days, Master Gerald," Nanny said.

Because it was such a characteristic remark, the Earl laughed.

He put his hand out to touch the Bible as he passed it.

"You can always pray, Nanny," he said lightly, "that she will drop down the chimney or out of the sky and I will fall in love at first sight!"

"Stranger things have happened, you mark my words!" Nanny said.

Then she said in a different tone:

"I can't wait to go next door and tell them what you've told me about the pensions. You won't forget, M'Lord?"

There was just a touch of anxiety in Nanny's voice, and the Earl said reassuringly:

"I shall remember, and I will not forget in the future to keep an eye on things myself. It is always a mistake to delegate authority."

Nanny opened the door for him, and then, because she looked touchingly courageous with her grey hair and her white apron, he bent and kissed her cheek.

"Good-bye, Nanny," he said. "You have helped me as I knew you would."

He turned away so as not to see the tears that suddenly misted her eyes, but by the time he drove off in his Chaise, she was waving to him and her smile had something youthful about it.

*   *   *

The Earl drove on to call, as Nanny had suggested, on one of his tenant-farmers.

What he learnt there made him so angry that the expression on his face when he returned to the Castle made the servants in the Hall look at him apprehensively.

"Send Mr. Aslett to me immediately!" he said to the Major-Domo.

He waited for his Agent in the Library, feeling a cold, calculated anger which he had not known for some years.

The words in which he dismissed the man who had defrauded those who had trusted him were as searingly caustic and as sharp as if he had used a whip across his shoulders.

When the Agent finally was allowed to leave the Earl, he walked as if he found it hard for his legs to carry him and his face as he walked out of the Castle for the last time was ashen.

Once he was rid of him, the Earl felt his good humour returning.

The anger he had expended on Aslett had given way to a satisfaction in knowing that he could right the wrongs that had been done, and in a most unexpected manner he had been able to unmask a swindler.

And yet, he told himself when he was alone, it was hardly to his own credit, but Ophelia's, that frail, lovely girl he had found unexpectedly and to whom he now owed a debt of gratitude.

If she had not spoken to him about Jem Bullet, he might have gone on for years trusting Aslett, as he trusted all those he employed, believing that his Pensioners, like his tenant-farmers, were properly content living in the shadow of the Castle.

His mother may have been a difficult, intensely Puritanical woman, but his father had been good-natured, generous, and a real country-gentleman.

He had administered his Estate in a kindly, fatherly manner, just as his father had done before him.

All the Wilmots, with the exception of himself, the Earl thought with a twist of his lips, had been rather stupid but thoroughly decent men.

The first Baronet, Sir Seymour Wilmot, who had served under Marlborough, had been beloved by his men and had been known throughout his Army career as "Jollyboy."

"However I might behave in my private life," the Earl told himself, "I am damned if I will neglect those who rely on me, those who up until now have trusted me."

He knew this only too well, for his father had taught him how those who worked on a great Estate were so vulnerable to the moods and foibles of their employer.

"It is like the Scots," Lord Wilmot had said solemnly to his small son, "who follow their Chieftain wherever he may lead them. They live for him and they will die for him!"

"Why do they do that?" the child had asked.

"Because, Gerald, a Chieftain is a father to the people who bear his name—the name of their Clan."

"But those who work for us are not called 'Wilmot.' "

"They still look to us for leadership, for security, and ultimately for happiness."

The Earl could remember his father's voice now, full of sincerity. He would have been a happy man had it not been for his wife.

"I will not make this sort of mistake another time," the Earl told himself.

'Strange how things work out!' his thoughts continued.

He had gone to George Langstone's house in Park Lane considering whether or not he would seduce his wife, and instead his daughter had, by a few frightened words, changed the lives of a great number of people.

Chapter Three

As he drove back to London, an uncomfortable thought suddenly struck the Earl.

He remembered over the years giving a number of instructions to his Comptroller, who was supposed to relay them to Aslett, and as he was in charge of all of the Earl's houses, he was expected to see that his orders were carried out.

This was certainly true regarding the old-age Pensioners, and the Earl now suspected that the Christmas presents he had ordered for them had not been delivered.

He did not for a moment suspect his Comptroller of being crooked and fraudulent as his Agent had been, but he realised that Mr. Gladwin, who was over sixty, had grown too old for the job.

The Earl was frank enough to admit that he was a very demanding person, and when he wanted something done, he wanted it at once. Gladwin was obviously finding it impossible to keep up with his personal demands and also cope with all his other duties.

There was a frown between the Earl's eyes and his lips were set in a hard line as he thought of the amount of trouble it would entail to start afresh with a new Comptroller.

At the same time, he was so appalled at what had happened on the Rochester Castle Estate that he knew he would have no peace of mind until everything he owned was administered more satisfactorily.

But to remove Gladwin would undoubtedly be a Herculean task.

Then an idea came to him, and before he reached

London he turned off the main road at Wimbledon Common.

He had remembered that an Officer with whom he had served in the Army lived in one of the small houses on the north side of the Common.

Several years older than the Earl himself, Major Musgrove had been his Adjutant and, he remembered, an extremely efficient one.

He had been in touch with him fairly recently over a reference for a man who had applied to him for employment and whose one claim to the position was that he had served with the Earl.

Major Musgrove's replies to the Earl's enquiries had been concise and, he discovered, accurate in every detail, and he thought at the time that he was the sort of person he would like to have in his own employment.

There was, of course, every chance that Major Musgrove had no wish to do anything but lead a quiet life of retirement. At the same time, the Earl was well aware that with the Treaty of Amiens an enormous number of officers and other men had been told that their services were no longer wanted.

These were, in many cases, forced into retirement at a far too early age.

He had spoken very forcefully in the House of Lords about the foolhardy way in which the Government was turning a blind eye to the fact that Napoleon was using the Armistice to regroup his forces and certainly to build more ships.

The Earl had in fact been very scathing, and he had even quoted some lines written by his namesake, the satirist:

> None's made great for being good and wise.
> Deserve a dungeon, if you would be great!
> Rogues always are our Ministers of State.

He had thought cynically that while the Ministers in question looked annoyed and embarrassed by the attack, nothing would be done.

The Earl was quite certain that the future would

justify his prophecy that England would soon be at war again, with a better-prepared France, having dissipated her own manpower and her weapons of war.

These thoughts, however, brought him back to Major Musgrove, and he drew up his horses beside an unpretentious little house, hoping almost against hope that Musgrove would agree to help him in what he considered an emergency in his day-to-day life!

Such a situation would greatly relieve his peace of mind.

*   *   *

Five days later, the Earl thought with almost a sense of embarrassment that he had still omitted to thank the person who was responsible for what, as far as he was concerned, had been a minor revolution.

In fact, everything had worked out far better than he had anticipated. Major Musgrove had jumped at the chance of having something worthwhile to do, especially with being entrusted with a task of reorganisation.

He understood everything that the Earl required, and had in fact been so tactful that no-one's feelings had been hurt, and from the moment he appeared, the machinery of the house in Berkeley Square seemed to revolve very much more efficiently.

What was so satisfactory was that Mr. Gladwin was only too pleased to retire.

"In fact, M'Lord," he said to the Earl, "I have been thinking I might do so for a long time."

The Earl thought his indecision was characteristic, and he made him a very generous gift of money which left his old Comptroller incoherent with gratitude.

Everything, the Earl thought now, was being tidied up in just the manner which he really appreciated.

But there was still just one loose end—called Ophelia.

He could not be so ungenerous, he told himself, not to thank her. At the same time, he wondered exactly how he could do so.

He was well aware, from the terror which she had

shown at their first meeting, that it would be quite impossible to arrive at Lord Langstone's house in Park Lane and ask to speak to her.

He was also certain that Circe would be exceedingly incensed even if, in some clever way, she was kept from knowing of his visit.

Then he knew that secrecy was completely impossible! Of course the servants would tell Lady Langstone that he had called, and Ophelia would suffer.

He had not, as it happened, seen Circe Langstone at any of the parties he attended on his return to London.

This was because they were either parties at which no lady would expect to be present, or else he was dining alone and intimately with Lady Harriet Sherwood.

At the same time, it was Lady Harriet who kept his thoughts returning to Circe Langstone.

It appeared that her brother was more infatuated than ever and that Circe was treating him so abominably that he was distraught almost to the point of suicide.

The Earl had an uneasy feeling that this might be due to his treatment of her!

Then he told himself that the idea was ridiculous: since he had only once been alone with Lady Langstone, and for a very short time, it could hardly have affected her to the point where she was venting her frustration on her lovers.

And yet women were unpredictable, and he knew only too well that Circe was a law unto herself.

He was, however, determined that he would somehow see Ophelia and that through her he would find out exactly what was happening in the Langstone household.

He deliberately drove down Park Lane two days running, hoping for a sight of the girl, but then he told himself that he was being absurd! He must either forget her or else take more positive steps to get in touch with her.

Unfortunately, he could not think how this could be,

and the next morning when he rode very early in the Park, he found himself still seriously considering what he could do.

The Earl liked riding early, before the Park was filled with women-riders, who tried to attract his attention, or with his men-friends, who tried to rival his horses with theirs.

Morning was the time of day when the Earl liked to be alone, and one of the reasons he was so athletically fit was that however late he might be out the night before, he was usually in the Park before seven.

The dew was still on the grass and there were only the gardeners already at work amongst the flower-beds.

He could gallop away the excesses of the night before and go home an hour later to eat a hearty breakfast.

Now he rode up Curzon Street towards Stanhope Gate, where the Park-Keeper, who lived in a very small pillared house, unlocked the gates at six o'clock in the morning.

The Earl was just about to cross Park Lane when he saw, inside the Park on the other side of the big iron gates, a slender figure.

For a moment he thought he must be imagining that it could be Ophelia; then as he waited to allow a lorry drawn by two slow horses to pass him, he realised that the girl in the white gown was undoubtedly the person he wished to see.

He saw that she had a brown and white spaniel on a lead, and it suddenly occurred to him that he had another point of contact with her that he had not thought of before.

Six months ago Mrs. Fitzherbert had beguiled the Prince into helping her collect money for a Hospital in which she was interested.

As usual, His Royal Highness, being hopelessly in debt, had little or nothing to give, but at Mrs. Fitzherbert's insistence he had asked his friends for their support.

There was a raffle to be held at the Ball given during the Cheltenham Races.

One or two people who wished to curry favour with the Heir to the Throne had given a horse, suggesting that such a valuable prize should not be included in the raffle but should be auctioned during the Ball.

The Earl, when asked by the Prince for a contribution, had no intention of parting with one of his precious horses, but he had in fact learnt only that very morning that one of his favourite spaniels at the Castle had produced a litter of six puppies.

This meant that the number of his dogs was getting out-of-hand.

There were six puppies from the previous year as well as the new litter, besides three dogs which were his special pets. He knew that he must give away either the new litter or some of those which were older.

It was not particularly generous of the Earl under the circumstances to offer one of his year-old spaniels, but Mrs. Fitzherbert had been delighted.

"I hear your dogs, My Lord, are famous for their good temper and sporting ability. In fact, I am quite certain that the spaniel you have given His Royal Highness will make a record amount for my charity."

Having ordered the dog to be handed over when it was asked for, the Earl had not thought about it again.

Now he remembered that the winner had in fact been Lord Langstone!

He crossed Park Lane and entered the Park, only to realise that the waggon had so delayed him that he had lost sight of Ophelia.

But he knew the direction in which she had been going and he found her some minutes later under the trees.

She was sitting, he noticed, in a rather hunched-up manner, with the spaniel beside her. She had let the dog off his lead but he was not running or frisking about, just sitting at her feet.

The Earl dismounted and, leading his horse by the bridle, walked towards her.

Obviously deep in her thoughts, she did not raise her head until he was standing beside her, and then she looked up casually as if expecting a stranger.

When she saw who stood there she gave a little cry

and the expression of terror he had seen once before
was back in her eyes.

"Good-morning, Miss Langstone . . ." the Earl began.

"Go . . . away! Please . . . go . . . away!" she cried.
"Do . . . not talk to . . . me! Please, leave me . . . alone."

The words seemed to come from her lips almost as
if she could not control them, and the Earl looked at
her in sheer astonishment before he asked:

"What is upsetting you? I only wish to speak to you
for a few moments."

As if his voice made her conscious of the strange
manner in which she was behaving, he saw her trying
to control herself. But he was aware that her whole
body was trembling before she said:

"Please . . . whatever you . . . have to say . . . say it
very . . . quickly."

As she finished speaking she glanced past the Earl
in the direction from which she had come, and he
remembered that it was the same manner in which she
had looked at the door of the Drawing-Room, as if
she thought her Stepmother was outside.

"If you are afraid of being seen with me," he said
quickly, "I suggest we walk a little farther into the
Park."

He knew that if they did so, they would be out of
sight of the house in Park Lane, although he thought
it was extremely unlikely that her Stepmother would
be looking out the window at this time of the morning.

Reluctantly, as if it was an effort to move, Ophelia
rose from the seat on which she had been sitting, and,
without saying anything, walked on amongst the trees
and the shrubs which were in bloom.

The Earl followed, leading his horse until they came
to a seat surrounded by rhododendrons and set back
from the path, where it would be impossible to be seen
except by someone standing directly in front of them.

Ophelia paused and the Earl said:

"I think this would suit us well. I would like you to sit
down and hear what I have to say."

She obeyed him as if she had not the spirit to argue,

and the Earl knotted his horse's reins on his neck and let him loose.

He was riding a stallion that was one of the oldest in his stables and of which he was very fond.

He had had Thunder since he was a foal and although he had been a wild, uncontrollable horse at one time in his life, he would now obey the Earl and come to him when he whistled.

The spaniel was crouched down at Ophelia's feet, and as the Earl sat down on the seat beside her he put out his hand towards the dog, saying:

"That is one of my dogs. What is his name?"

But before he could touch it, the spaniel gave a little yelp and cringed under the seat in fear.

The Earl looked surprised, then asked:

"Why is the dog so nervous? I have never known any of my breed to be afraid."

"It is . . . because you have a . . . riding . . . whip in your . . . hand," Ophelia said in a low voice.

The Earl put his whip down on the seat and then he asked:

"Are you telling me my dog has been whipped until he is afraid? But why, and for what reason?"

There was a peremptory note in his voice, because if the Earl had one obsession it was against cruelty.

One of his wild exploits which had gained him a great deal of publicity was when he had half-killed a waggon-driver whom he had seen being cruel to his horse.

He had fought the man in the open street, the spectators making a ring round them, and when he had knocked him down, he had proceeded to thrash him with the whip he had used on the horse.

While many people approved of his action, a great many of his contemporaries thought it was vulgar behaviour on the part of a gentleman, and on the whole the Earl had a worse reputation after the incident than he had had before it.

Now without his whip, he bent down to coax the spaniel, as it cowered against Ophelia, until he could lift it in his arms.

Then, putting it on his knee, he stroked its head until finally the dog, with its instinctive desire to be made a fuss of, nuzzled against him.

He did not speak all the time he was caressing the spaniel, as he knew that his voice might frighten him. However, when finally he felt that the spaniel was no longer afraid, he said quietly to Ophelia:

"This dog is much too thin, for I can feel his bones, and he is obviously not having enough to eat."

There was silence until finally Ophelia said in an unhappy little voice:

"I . . . can do . . . nothing about . . . it."

"I cannot believe that your father . . ." the Earl began angrily.

Then as he looked at Ophelia, he noticed a difference in her.

The last time he had seen her, which was less than a week ago, she had been lovely in an unusual manner which he had found impossible to forget. But now he saw that she was very much thinner than she had been then.

Her eyes seemed enormous in her face and there were blue lines beneath them which had certainly not been there before.

"What has happened to you?" he asked gently. "Have you been ill?"

He saw her shiver and then he said:

"If this dog has had too little to eat, it is obvious that the same applies to you. What have you been doing to yourself?"

It flashed through his mind that perhaps she had been slimming herself to be fashionable.

It was what a great number of women had been doing since the design of the new straight muslin gowns which had originated in Paris had come to London.

These muslins were practically transparent and some of the women dampened them to reveal the slim perfections of their figures. But even as the thought occurred to him, he knew it was absurd.

Ophelia's slimness and grace the first time he had seen her were the result of youth.

She did not speak for a moment and then she answered:

"There is no ... point in Your Lordship asking such ... questions. Please tell me what you ... want to say ... quickly and then ... leave me. I do not think ... I can ... stand ... any ... more."

The last words came out almost involuntarily and the Earl said quietly:

"Stand what? Listen, Ophelia, I want to know what is happening both to you and to this dog, and I intend to learn the truth!"

He saw her clasp her hands together as if with an effort to prevent herself from crying out at his insistence, or perhaps to prevent herself from running away.

He knew that she was afraid to the point where her whole body was tense.

"Let us talk about the dog first," he said. "What is his name?"

"Rover. He was called ... Rover when Papa ... won him," Ophelia said in a low voice.

The Earl smiled.

"That is understandable. All my dogs' names start with an *R*, and to tell you the truth, I am running short of them!"

He hoped she would smile at his explanation, but he knew, although she was no longer looking at him, that her eyes were dark with fear and also, he thought, with a resentment because he insisted on cross-examining her.

The Earl was accustomed to any woman he talked to responding to him immediately, and it was a novel sensation to know that the girl by his side wanted more than anything in the world for him to go away and leave her alone.

Obstinately he was determined that he would not go until he found out what all this peculiar behaviour meant. And particularly until he learnt who had been beating one of his dogs.

He was just about to ask another question when Ophelia said in a different tone:

"I should have ... thanked you, My Lord, for what

you . . . have done for Jem Bullet. I . . . it . . . was rude
of me not to have . . . mentioned it at once."

"I am glad you are pleased," the Earl said with just
a touch of sarcasm in his voice.

"I am much more than . . . pleased," Ophelia said. "It
haunted me that he had been without . . . food, and
living in that terrible . . . house in Lambeth."

"Who told you of Jem Bullet's circumstances?"

"His daughter," Ophelia replied. "She is an . . . under-housemaid at . . . home, and I went with her to . . .
see her father, which is . . . how I knew he had not . . .
received his pension."

"I could not believe it was true when you told me he
had been neglected in such a way," the Earl replied.
"That was really the reason I wished to see you,
Ophelia—to thank you for giving me the opportunity
to put right what was undoubtedly a grave wrong."

"You did not . . . mean to . . . leave him . . . penniless?"

As she spoke, she turned to look at the Earl as if
she wanted to make sure for herself that he was telling
the truth.

"After what you had told me," the Earl said quietly,
"I went to the country and discovered that my Agent
had been defrauding the old-age Pensioners; he was
taking for himself money I had allotted for their pensions."

He saw a sudden light come into Ophelia's eyes and
he thought also that a faint colour just tinged the
whiteness of her pale cheeks.

"Oh! I am so glad!" she exclaimed. "So very glad you
did not . . . deliberately make the poor old man . . . suffer."

The Earl felt a sudden wave of anger.

"Whatever stories you have heard about me, Miss
Langstone, I do not starve those who have served me,
when they retire either from old age or injury."

"I . . . am . . . sorry," Ophelia said quickly. "I am . . .
sorry, I did not . . . mean to make you so . . . angry, but
it seemed strange that . . . you should have behaved in
such a . . . manner."

A Personal Invitation from Barbara Cartland

Dear Reader,

I have formed the Barbara Cartland "Health and Happiness Club" so that I can share with you my sensational discoveries on beauty, health, love and romance, which is both physical and spiritual.

I will communicate with you through a series of newsletters throughout the year which will serve as a forum for you to tell me what you personally have felt, and you will also be able to learn the thoughts and feelings of other members who join me in my "Search for Rainbows." I will be thrilled to know you wish to participate.

In addition, the Health and Happiness Club will make available to members only, the finest quality health and beauty care products personally selected by me.

Do please join my Health and Happiness Club. Together we will find the secrets which bring rapture and ecstasy to my heroines and point the way to true happiness.

Yours,

FREE Membership Offer
Health
&
Happiness Club

Dear Barbara,

Please enroll me as a charter member in the Barbara Cartland "Health and Happiness Club." My membership application appears on the form below (or on a plain piece of paper).

I look forward to receiving the first in a series of your newsletters and learning about your sensational discoveries on beauty, health, love and romance.

I understand that the newsletters and membership in your club are _free_.

* * *

Kindly send your membership application to:
Health and Happiness Club, Inc.
Two Penn Plaza
New York, N.Y. 10001

NAME_____

ADDRESS_____

CITY_____STATE____ZIP_____

Allow 2 weeks for delivery of the first newsletter.

Her voice pleaded with him to understand as she continued:

"Jem Bullet actually went to see your Agent when he could walk after his ... accident, who told him that you were very ... close-fisted with those who could no longer be of any use to you."

"May I inform you that that is an absolute and complete lie, and I hope you believe me."

"I do! I do now," Ophelia said. "It was only that I was so upset by Jem Bullet's circumstances, and I know that some people can be very ... cruel."

There was a note in her voice which told the Earl that now she was speaking personally, and as his hand fondled the dog on his knee, he said:

"Just as you worried about my old groom, I am worrying about this dog, which I still think of as mine."

"There is ... nothing you can ... do," Ophelia said quietly. "Though perhaps you could ask Papa to ... allow you to have him ... back."

"That would be rather a difficult thing to do," the Earl replied, "without giving a reason for it. Shall I tell your father that I think he is being ill-treated?"

Ophelia gave a little cry of sheer terror.

"No! No! Please ... do not do ... that! Promise me ... you will not say ... anything to Papa. If she ..."

She stopped suddenly.

"What were you going to say about your Stepmother?" the Earl asked.

There was a silence and he waited.

Ophelia was no longer looking at him, but he watched her profile and he knew she was considering what she should say and whether she should trust him.

Then suddenly she made up her mind.

"Could you please ... go and see ... Stepmama? Could you call ... on ... her? Could you be ... nice to ... her?"

There was something in the way that Ophelia said "nice" which made the Earl look at her now even more searchingly.

Then he asked:

"And if I do? Will that stop her from beating Rover?"

It was a bow at a venture, and yet when he said it, he knew he had touched on the truth, for Ophelia's eyes flickered and now there was a faint flush on her pale cheeks.

Because of the way she looked and because too of an instinct within himself where she was concerned, which he could not understand, he said:

"And has she also been beating you? Is that why you look as you do?"

Now the colour flooded crimson into her face, then ebbed away, leaving her paler than she had been before.

The Earl said:

"Answer me, Ophelia! I want to know! Tell me what has been happening."

For a moment he thought she would refuse to answer. Then in a voice so low he could hardly hear, she said:

"She ... thought it was my ... fault that you ... went away so very ... quickly the day you ... called."

"And she has beaten you because of that?" the Earl asked incredulously.

"Every ... day," Ophelia whispered.

"And Rover?"

"Because ... she knows it ... upsets me ... and we are ... both of us only ... allowed ... bread and water."

The Earl put his hand up to his forehead.

"I can hardly credit that what you are telling me is the truth!"

Yet he knew that what he was saying was only words, and he could see with his eyes that what Ophelia was telling him was true.

Now once again she turned to look at him and her eyes seemed to have just a faint hope in them.

"Please ... do what ... Stepmama wants," she begged.

The Earl thought that never in the whole of his life had he found himself in such a strange, almost unbelievable predicament.

If he refused, which was his immediate instinct, knowing that what he had heard about Circe Langstone disgusted him, then he was condemning this child and one of his own dogs to a purgatory that was too bestial to contemplate.

He found himself thinking that with a daily beating and a diet of bread and water, neither of them would live very long, and perhaps their death was exactly what Lady Langstone intended.

He had heard Lady Harriet raving against Circe so violently and so often that the Earl had grown used to thinking that, like most women, Harriet exaggerated.

No-one could be as bad or as evil as she was making out Circe Langstone to be. But now he was aware that she was even worse than Harriet or anyone else imagined!

He realised that Ophelia was waiting anxiously for his reply.

"Whatever else I do," the Earl said, "I must save you from the position you are in at the moment."

"Only . . . you can do . . . that," she answered quietly.

"Supposing I spoke to your father?"

Ophelia made a little helpless gesture which at the same time had a grace, the Earl thought, and which made her hands seem like the movements of the little flies hovering over the rhododendron blossoms.

"Papa will not . . . listen," she said. "He believes everything Stepmother tells him."

"He must see that you are looking ill and how thin you have grown," the Earl insisted.

"Stepmama tells him that it is my own fault, that I will not eat the food that is provided, and that I spend my nights reading instead of sleeping."

The Earl thought he had always known that George Langstone was a fool, but that did not get him any further in finding a solution to the problem.

"Could you . . . please take . . . Rover away . . . somehow?" Ophelia asked. "He is such a dear little dog . . . so trusting and loving. He does not . . . understand why he is being . . . beaten."

There was a throb in her voice which the Earl found very moving.

"And what about you?" he asked.

"I . . . I . . . shall be . . . all right."

"Looking at you, I think that is the last thing you are likely to be," the Earl said drily. "Surely you have relations you can go to?"

"I have thought about that," Ophelia replied, "but I think Stepmama would . . . have me . . . brought back."

"Why?"

"Because she would be . . . afraid they would . . . introduce me to their friends, that I would meet people at their house. She does not want anyone to know that I even . . . exist."

"That is ridiculous!" the Earl said. "Of course you exist, and there must be some of your relatives who realise that you are grown up and should have been presented this Season."

"If they have enquired about me," Ophelia replied, "I have not been told about it."

The Earl thought it was like finding himself in the Hampton Court Maze without having the least idea as to how to get out!

All the time he was talking to Ophelia, he was thinking of what he should do and how he could save this pathetic child and most certainly his own dog.

The obvious course, he told himself firmly, was to tackle George Langstone, but even as he decided that that was what he must do, he saw Circe's eyes green and provocative, inveigling smile.

The Earl knew that Langstone would be far too besotted with his second wife to listen to anything that might be said against her.

When it came to a choice between the woman he desired and his daughter, it was obvious who would win!

'I have to do something,' the Earl thought to himself, and knew that as far as Ophelia was concerned, it would have to be soon.

"Are you quite seriously telling me," he said aloud, "that if I come to see your Stepmother today, as apparently she still wants me to do, you and Rover will not be beaten tonight?"

"She might . . . not do so if you . . . you made her . . . happy," Ophelia said.

The Earl was well aware of what she meant by the

word "happy," and once again he thought that of all
the extraordinary propositions he had ever had in his
life, and there had been a large number, he had never
yet had someone as young and as beautiful as Ophelia
pleading with him to make love to another woman.

Even as he thought of it, he knew it would be impossible after what he had learnt for him to touch Circe
Langstone, let alone make love to her.

Every instinct in him was appalled by a woman who
could be cruel in the manner she had been, first to anything as fragile as Ophelia, and secondly to an animal.

"Please," Ophelia repeated.

The Earl had the sudden feeling that the dog in his
arms was adding his plea to hers. He made up his mind.

"I will call on your Stepmother this afternoon, on one
condition."

"What is . . . that?" Ophelia asked.

"That you will meet me here tomorrow morning at
the same time."

She looked at him wide-eyed before she said:

"I had much . . . better not see you . . . again. It was
because I talked to you that all . . . this happened . . . in
the first place."

"Because this has happened," the Earl said firmly, "I
insist on seeing you in the morning. That is my condition, Ophelia. If you refuse me, then I may have other
things to do this afternoon."

He knew he was being almost brutal in his insistence
that they should meet.

But at the same time, remembering how afraid he
had been that he would never get in touch with her, he
knew it was the only way he could ensure that he would
learn what had occurred after his visit.

Moreover, he felt a responsibility both to Ophelia and
to Rover.

Ostensibly it was because of him that they had suffered the way they had, and he knew that just as he had
been incensed by the way his old-age Pensioners had
suffered, he was now incensed to the point of a cold
calculating anger that Circe should have behaved in
such an appalling manner.

Ophelia had suddenly become the object of a crusade that he was determined to win in one way or another.

At the same time, he was already aware that he had no intention of doing exactly what she asked of him, though how he could find an alternative way of placating Circe was a different question altogether.

"I will . . . meet you here . . . as you have . . . asked me to do," Ophelia said with a little sigh.

"You promise?" the Earl insisted.

"I promise."

"And let me make sure you do not break your promise by saying I will bring you some food."

"And some for Rover?"

"And some for Rover," he agreed.

He suddenly thought that as she looked so frail she might not last even until tomorrow.

"Surely someone in the house will give you something to eat today?" he asked.

"They have all been forbidden to do so," Ophelia answered, "but I think Rover sometimes steals off the table when he has the chance."

"Let me return to my house and get you something now," the Earl suggested.

Ophelia shook her head.

"I had better go back. Stepmama's lady's-maid will notice if I am away for a long time. She spies on me. It was she who told Stepmama that I had . . . spoken to you in the Drawing-Room."

The situation was intolerable, the Earl told himself. However, he knew that women like Circe always had servants who would spy for them and in whom they confided.

A *complice d'amour* was what the French called it, but he could think of nastier and more unpleasant descriptions.

Ophelia rose.

"You must . . . go on with your . . . ride."

She looked away from him to where Thunder was cropping the grass.

"He is a magnificent horse," she said almost beneath her breath.

"You like horses?" the Earl asked.

"Mama and I used to ride together when she was alive, and we were very happy."

There was something pathetic in the way she spoke, as if happiness was in the past and she would never know it again.

The Earl thought that he would like to put her on one of his horses and gallop with her across the Park at the Castle.

Then he told himself that, while trying to save Ophelia from the tortures her Stepmother was inflicting on her, he must certainly not become embroiled with a young girl, if for no other reason than that her reputation would suffer because of it.

Ophelia was in fact right in saying that he must go on with his ride and she must go home. Time was getting on.

Soon there would be other riders coming into the Park, and the Earl knew that he was too well-known for them not to ask questions about anyone to whom he was seen talking.

"I will see you tomorrow," he said.

He smiled at her as if she were a child who needed encouraging, then mounted Thunder.

Astride the big stallion, when he looked down at Ophelia she looked very small, insubstantial, and immature.

'How can she cope with the world in which she is living?' the Earl wondered to himself.

She turned her face up to his, and her eyes spoke even more plainly than her lips as she asked:

"You will be very . . . careful what you . . . say?"

"Trust me," the Earl replied. "Trust me, Ophelia. I will try not to let you down."

"I do . . . trust you," she answered.

The words were so low that he could hardly hear them, and then she turned and walked back the way they had come, with Rover following her.

The Earl watched her for a few seconds; then, as he deliberately spurred Thunder into a gallop over the rough ground beside the Serpentine, he found the same questions repeating themselves over and over again in his mind:

"What the devil is to be done about her?

"What the devil can I do?"

*　　*　　*

Circe Langstone stepped out of her carriage and, followed by Marie, entered the house.

She was looking very spectacular in a bonnet trimmed with green ostrich-feathers and a green taffeta pelisse to cover her green gown.

There was a sulky look about her face and she ignored the bowing flunkeys and the Butler who stepped forward, obviously to speak to her.

She had in fact started to climb the staircase before Bateson said:

"The Earl of Rochester, M'Lady, has called."

Lady Langstone turned her head as if she thought she could not have heard him aright.

"What?" she enquired.

"The Earl of Rochester is waiting for Your Ladyship in the Drawing-Room."

For a moment Circe did not move, and then without a word she hurried up the staircase, followed by Marie.

Only as the door of her bedroom shut behind her did she say:

"He's come, so Zenobe was right!"

"I told you, M'Lady, I told you," Marie said, "you could trust her! That spell is infallible! I have told you before it works, it always works!"

Marie had spoken in French, in which she always conversed with her Mistress when they were afraid of being overheard.

Circe, however, spoke English as she said:

"He has come! And now, Marie, I must hold him— he must not escape!"

"Trust in Zenobe, M'Lady!"

"I do! I do!" Circe cried.

As she was speaking, she flung off her bonnet and pelisse, then glanced at herself in the mirror to see if she should change. But she was too impatient, and the green gown she was wearing was in fact one of her very latest purchases.

It clung to her figure in the prescribed fashion and

gave the impression that she was naked beneath it, which she was!

But Circe was too clever to be completely blatant, as many other women contrived to be. Her gown suggested rather than revealed, and her sinuous, feline body did the rest.

Because she was concentrating, using the power that she knew no man could resist, she moved slowly along the passage towards the Drawing-Room.

Then as the flunkey opened the door, she took a deep breath. The Earl was standing by the window, looking out over Park Lane towards the Park.

He was thinking of the extraordinary conversation he had had that morning with Ophelia and finding it hard to believe everything she had told him, even though he knew it was the truth.

He thought of every possible way in which he could extricate himself from the position into which not deliberately but pathetically she had put him, but he had known there was nothing he could do except call on Circe Langstone.

He was, however, astute enough to have thought out some sort of plan before he arrived at George Langstone's house, and as the door opened and he saw Circe standing there, he found himself wondering almost frantically if it would work.

"This is a delightful surprise, My Lord."

Circe Langstone spoke in a silky voice which, the Earl thought, matched her movements.

As she walked towards him now, he was reminded even more forcefully than before that she was like a serpent.

She held out her hand and he bowed over it. He did not kiss it as he was quite certain she had intended him to do.

"Do sit down, My Lord," she said with a smile. "I hope today your horses are not waiting for you impatiently as they were last time you came here."

"I was hoping you would give me the pleasure of letting me drive you in the Park."

The Earl thought, as he spoke, that this was something she might not be able to resist because she could show him off to her friends and they would assume immediately that he was caught in her toils.

He had, however, underestimated his opponent!

Circe smiled almost as if she sensed that by what he was suggesting, he was evading the main issue.

"I have just returned from a drive," she said, "and quite frankly I would rather rest and talk to you."

"Then I have another suggestion to make."

"What is that?"

"That you should dine with me tomorrow night."

Circe raised her eye-brows. It was obviously an invitation she had not expected.

"Are you having a party?" she asked. "Or shall we be alone?"

"That, of course, is entirely up to Your Ladyship," the Earl replied. "I would like you to see my house."

He said it in a manner which made the words suggest a special meaning.

It occurred to Circe for the first time that the reason he had not made love to her as she had hoped on the afternoon he had first called upon her was that he was too fastidious to deceive any man in his own house!

None of her lovers had ever felt such scruples, so she had never considered that the Earl might feel that such behaviour was a breach of good taste or perhaps of sportsmanship.

Now she thought that she had been extremely insensitive in not realising before that despite his raffish reputation, he was, above all things, a great gentleman.

There were few men of whom she could say the same thing, but there was an air of consequence about the Earl which told her that she could not expect to treat him as she had treated the rabble who fell so easily at her feet and certainly had no scruples about deceiving her husband.

She was so elated at finding out what she thought was the real reason for his previous unexpected behaviour that she rebuked herself later for accepting his invitation far too quickly.

"I shall be delighted to dine with you, My Lord," she said before she could prevent herself.

"That is what I should be saying," the Earl replied,

"and I only hope your husband will not think I am extremely remiss in not including him in the invitation."

Again Circe smiled.

"On such occasions I always tell George," she said softly, "that I am dining with a friend to listen to a concert. If there is one thing which really bores him, it is music."

The Earl managed to laugh.

"Then, so that we can be truthful, I will promise you music. The sort that we can hear but not see!"

"That will be delightful and very ... romantic?"

There was just a slight pause before the last word, which made it a question.

The Earl smiled and rose to his feet.

"Then I shall expect you tomorrow night, My Lady, at half-after-seven. I dine at the same time as His Royal Highness."

It was the fashionable hour and very much later than most ordinary people, who started dinner usually an hour or at least half-an-hour earlier.

Circe put out her hand, and this time it was the one which bore the huge emerald.

The Earl looked down at the stone, thinking that in its depths there was the same evil as in its owner's eyes.

"You are admiring my ring?" Circe enquired.

"And the hand that wears it," the Earl said automatically.

He knew that if he played his part correctly, he would then kiss her hand. But he could not bring himself to do so.

Even to touch Circe Langstone was to experience something so repulsive that it affected him even more violently than the cobra he had once thought she resembled.

He made what was almost a Court bow and then released her, but he managed to say with an unmistakable meaning behind the words:

"Until tomorrow night."

As he left the room he did not look back but walked slowly down the stairs with the undeniable dignity that was habitual to him.

Only as he reached the Hall did he find that he al-most had to repress an instinct to run and keep on run-ning.

Never, he told himself as he stepped into his Phaeton that was waiting outside, had he been aware that all the forces of Satan could be concentrated in the body of one woman.

Chapter Four

Ophelia went home feeling that everything would be all right because she could trust the Earl.

There were quite a lot of things for her to do that day. Fortunately they were all in the house, for her legs felt so weak that she thought that if she went outside they would no longer support her.

She knew that it was caused by a lack of food, and her back from her Stepmother's continual beating was like a burning fire.

By five o'clock she was so exhausted that she crawled upstairs to her bedroom, knowing that she could do no more.

On the table inside her room were three slices of bread and a pitcher of water.

There was nothing for Rover, and she was well aware that her Stepmother, with her crafty mind, knew that she gave to the little dog most of the food she was expected to eat herself.

It had been a very subtle way of punishing her, to make Rover suffer too, and as he looked eagerly up at the bread, she broke it up into small pieces for him, soaked some of it in the water, and put it on a plate on the floor.

He gobbled it up in a few seconds, then looked at her expectantly.

"There is no more," she said, "but perhaps we will get something later on."

She knew that this was a forlorn hope.

Even though the Earl had called, she suspected that her Stepmother would go on with her punishments just because she hated her.

It was unfortunate that her father had been away for the last three days at Epsom, where he was inspecting his race-horses and staying with some friends.

The night before he left, Ophelia had made up her mind to tell him of the way her Stepmother was treating her.

After all, if he saw her back and the criss-cross weals that were bleeding from the thin riding-whip that Circe used so vigorously, when faced with such evidence her father could not pretend to believe his wife's lies.

Yet, everything that was sensitive in Ophelia shrank from bringing her father into the war that existed between herself and her Stepmother.

She knew how much he hated scenes, and she felt too that if he really knew what sort of woman he had put in her mother's place, it would somehow damage the memory he had of the wife he had loved for so many years.

It was all rather complicated in Ophelia's mind.

At the same time, the humiliation she suffered at her Stepmother's hands was something she could not bear to speak of, and it was only because the Earl had so positively insisted on knowing the truth that she had told him as much as she had.

Now because she felt so weak she took a bite of the slice of bread that was left, and found it was dry and stuck in her throat.

Impulsively she broke the rest of it into small pieces and gave it to Rover; then, moving towards her bed, she lay down on it and closed her eyes.

She was half-unconscious rather than dreaming when there was a faint knock on the door and Emily came in.

She shut the door carefully behind her before she hurried to the bedside.

"I've brought you somethin' to eat, Miss Ophelia," she said. " 'Tis not much, but it's cheese and a weeny bit o' chicken I snatched from the table when the Chef weren't looking."

For a moment Ophelia felt too weak to move.

Then because she knew how hard it was for Emily to help her, she forced herself to sit up.

"Thank you . . . Emily," she said. "What about . . . Rover?"

"I've something for him too," Emily said, proudly

feeling in the pocket of her apron and producing a piece of newspaper.

When she put it down on the floor Ophelia could see that it was filled with scraps that she guessed had been left on the servants' plates at luncheon and which had been consigned to the dustbin.

Rover, however, was not particular. He gobbled up every particle, and for the first time in days, his tail was wagging.

"Thank you, Emily," Ophelia said gratefully.

"Now eat what I've brought you, Miss Ophelia. You looks half-dead, and that's a fact!"

"And that is how I feel," Ophelia answered.

Because she knew it would please Emily, she ate the small piece of chicken and tried to swallow some of the cheese.

It took quite an effort on her part, and only because Emily poured her out some water did she manage to wash it down.

For the first two days on bread and water she had felt desperately hungry, with an aching void inside her. After that, she only felt weak and it was difficult even to swallow the bread that was brought up morning and evening by one of the servants.

That was an humiliation in itself, but Ophelia was past caring. All she worried about was Rover and the fact that her Stepmother beat him deliberately to upset her.

"I cannot eat . . . any more," she said now to Emily.

There was only a small amount of cheese left, little bigger than a piece which would bait a mouse-trap.

Emily picked it up as if it were precious and looked round the room for somewhere to conceal it.

"I am very grateful," Ophelia said; "it is a meal I shall remember."

"But now you will have to pay for it!" a sharp voice said from the doorway.

As both of the girls started in sheer terror, Circe came into the room.

*　　*　　*

The Earl spent a most enjoyable evening at Carlton House.

It was the sort of dinner-party he liked, when the Prince of Wales was in his most scintillating form and the conversation was both witty and stimulating.

No-one could be a more genial host and no-one could in fact be more amusing than the Prince, when he did not drink too much.

He was not only extremely well-educated and had exceptionally good taste, but he also had a witty turn of phrase and was able to mimic people in a manner which was quite exceptional.

In fact, it had often been said that had he been obliged to earn his own living, he would have been a huge success in the Playhouse.

Besides the Prince, there was Charles Fox, who, although he was dirty and a compulsive gambler, had without exception the most brilliant brain in Parliament.

Another of the guests was Lord Alvanley, who was acclaimed as a wit, and a number of other men, all of whom had some special qualifications for being present.

The food was superb, the wines were excellent, and when the Prince intimated that he wished to retire, it was still not yet midnight.

It was Mrs. Fitzherbert who, having returned to the Prince after his disastrous marriage, had persuaded him not only to restrict his drinking but also to give up the late hours he had been keeping, which the Doctors alleged over and over again were bad for his health.

There was no point in asking Charles Fox where he was going, for he would instinctively make for the gaming-tables, where he would sit until dawn, losing money he could ill afford.

The Earl had been told by a number of his friends that on average he lost five hundred guineas a night.

Lord Alvanley, who could seldom afford to gamble, was going to White's, where he would find a number of his cronies drinking and, if they were not too drunk, also gambling.

Another guest suggested to the Earl that they should visit one of the "Houses of Pleasure" which flourished all round St. James's.

"I hear a new batch of French Cypriots have arrived in the last few days," he said. "We should certainly pay them a visit. Come with me, Rake."

He looked surprised when the Earl replied:

"Not tonight. I want to go home."

His friend raised his eye-brows.

"Is that a polite word for some fair charmer?"

"As it happens, it is just the simple truth," the Earl replied.

His friend shook his head.

"If you are not careful, Rake, you will be losing your reputation as the most bawdy man in town."

"That, of course, would be a disaster!" the Earl replied sarcastically, and his friend laughed.

"I will give you a personal report on what the 'pieces o' muslin' from across the Channel are like," he promised.

"I never enjoy my pleasures vicariously," the Earl replied, and his friend laughed again.

Because it was a pleasant, warm night, with the moon high in the sky, the Earl sent away his closed carriage, which was waiting for him, and walked from Carlton House up St. James's Street towards Berkeley Square.

He was so deep in his thoughts that several loose women who would have tried to attract his attention stepped back as he passed them, as if they realised that he was unaware of their very existence.

The exercise, however, after the large dinner he had eaten at Carlton House, pleased him.

Only as he reached his own front door did he wonder if in fact it had been a mistake to return home so early.

He had thought he wanted to think, but now he felt that his own thoughts were too worrying for him to have any chance of sleeping or even resting.

Ever since he had left Circe he had known he had two problems which had to be solved: the first, how to cancel the invitation he had given her to dinner; the second, and by far the most important, how to get Ophelia out of her clutches.

He tried to remember who he knew amongst the Langstone relations and drew a blank.

George Langstone was not an important nobleman

and he moved in the highest Society only because he was wealthy and a sportsman.

When the Social Code had been more stringent, the Earl knew, George Langstone, who came from the North, would not have been accepted.

The Prince of Wales had widened the boundaries of those who were in the *Beau Monde* because of the very strange and often disreputable persons he himself called his friends.

It was not surprising that the King and Queen looked askance at those who were entertained at Carlton House.

At the same time, because the Prince's friends were so much more amusing than his father's and mother's, when the great hostesses invited him, they were forced to include almost all his favourites.

"There must be somebody who can help me," the Earl said to himself irritably.

It was ridiculous to think that he, an avowed bachelor, a man who never, if he could possibly avoid it, spoke to a young girl, should find himself embroiled in a tangle with one in a manner that for the moment seemed so twisted that he could not find a way to unravel it.

One answer was, of course, simply to walk away and let things take care of themselves.

What did it matter to him if Ophelia, whom he had only set eyes on twice in his life, was beaten into a pulp by her Stepmother? And if the same thing happened to a dog he had once owned, he had a great number of others.

Then he knew that however badly he had behaved in his own life up to now, and however wicked quite a number of people might think him to be, he had never willingly harmed anything helpless and vulnerable which could not defend itself.

The women he had loved and left weeping had all been sophisticated and worldly, with a complete awareness of the risks they took in allowing him to become their lover.

He knew that at times he treated them harshly and

that there were incidents in his past which he would rather not remember.

But never, and this was the truth, had he ever stood by and watched a child or an animal ill-treated, and he was certainly not going to begin now.

He raised his hand to the polished knocker on his own door, and when it was opened by the night-footman he walked in, handing a second flunkey his hat and evening-cape.

He would have walked into the Library when his Butler, who had been with him for many years, came into the Hall to say:

"Excuse me, M'Lord, but there's a young woman here who wishes to see you."

"A young woman?" the Earl exclaimed.

It flashed through his mind that it might be Ophelia. Then he knew that such a thing was impossible.

"She's a servant-girl, M'Lord," the Butler explained, "and she asked me to tell you she's Jem Bullet's daughter and 'twas very important that she should speak with Your Lordship."

Jem Bullet's daughter!

The Earl remembered Ophelia telling him that she was an under-housemaid in her father's employment.

"I will see her," the Earl said, and walked into the Library.

There was an open bottle of champagne waiting for him on the grog-tray, but he was not thirsty, only intensely curious as to why Bullet's daughter should come to see him at this hour of the night.

As he waited, it struck him that this might be another problem for him to solve, and with a tightening of his lips he thought that he was certainly beset by them.

How could he have imagined a week ago that through one short conversation his well-ordered life would be disrupted to the extent where he had been obliged to replace his Agent and his Comptroller?

Furthermore, he now found himself occupied not with the enticements of his mistresses but with difficulties which reminded him of the part he had played at the time of the French Revolution.

Then his quick thinking and a talent for disguise had not only saved his own life a dozen times, but allowed him to save a great number of others as well.

The excitement he had felt then he had, in the last few years, accepted as being lost with his youth.

Now those feelings were back again and he recognised them.

They were always the same just before something happened.

He felt as if the curtain was rising and unless he could act the part to perfection without making a single slip, then there would not be applause but consequences to which he dared not put a name.

The door of the Library opened.

"Emily Bullet, M'Lord!" the Butler announced.

Emily came into the room and bobbed a curtsey.

She looked extremely nervous, but the Earl liked what he saw.

She was obviously a country-girl, thickly built, with a round, apple-cheeked face and honest, rather shy eyes. She wore a black dress and round her shoulders was a woollen shawl.

She had a small straw bonnet with ribbons tied under her chin.

They were the type of clothes that every respectable servant-girl wore for best and which he had seen ever since his boyhood when the maid-servants walked on Sundays down the drive of the Castle to the village Church, where they worshipped.

Emily was standing just inside the Library door and the Earl thought there was a beseeching look in her eyes.

"You are Jem Bullet's daughter?" he asked.

"Yes, M'Lord."

"Why have you come to see me?"

"Miss Ophelia sent me, an', M'Lord, I didn't wish to trouble you, but she says I were to come."

"Why?" the Earl enquired.

"Her Ladyship turned me out o' the house tonight without a reference, and I've no money, M'Lord, not a penny!"

Emily's voice broke and the Earl saw that she was very near to tears.

"Will you come a little nearer to me," he asked quietly, "and tell me exactly what happened? Why did Her Ladyship turn you out?"

" 'Twas because I took Miss Ophelia an' the little dog somethin' to eat, M'Lord. I knowed 'twas wrong of me after I'd been told not to, but they was both starving, M'Lord, an' I couldn't get anythin' to her afore 'cause I were being watched."

The Earl did not speak, and Emily, as if she thought he did not understand, said:

"Miss Ophelia's being punished, M'Lord. Tonight 'twas terrible, and I thinks Her Ladyship had killed her!"

"Killed her?"

The Earl's question seemed to ring out.

"Yes, M'Lord. She was unconscious when I leaves th' room, but when I went back, she spoke to me an' told I to come to you."

"Are you telling me," the Earl asked, in a deliberately controlled voice, "that Her Ladyship beat Miss Ophelia tonight?"

"Yes, M'Lord, an' she made me watch her do it, because I'd taken Miss Ophelia somethin' to eat."

"What happened?" the Earl asked.

It was difficult for him to keep the anger out of his voice, but, knowing that it would frighten Emily more than she was already, he managed to speak very quietly.

"I takes Miss Ophelia up a bit o' cheese an' chicken, M'Lord," Emily said, "an' some scraps for th' dog."

"That was kind of you."

"I knowed I'd get into trouble if I were caught, but I thinks I were safe enough, as we'd been told Her Ladyship was lying down an' the French maid who tells her everythin' were with her."

"Go on," the Earl prompted.

"Well, Miss Ophelia eats what I gives her an' the little dog just gobbles it up, then Her Ladyship comes into the room. Oh, M'Lord, 'twere horrible!"

Emily was crying now.

She pulled out a handkerchief from her sleeve and hid her eyes in it.

The Earl waited for a moment, then said:

"I want you to tell me everything that happened, then perhaps I can do something about it."

" 'Tis too late now," Emily said, sobbing. "Miss Ophelia'll die! I thinks her were dead tonight, I did really! There were blood all over her back, but I couldn't look. I couldn't, M'Lord!"

"And Her Ladyship also beat the dog?" the Earl asked.

"Thrashed him, she did, M'Lord, till he yelped an' screamed almost like a child! An' Miss Ophelia kept crying: 'Hit me, but not Rover! He doesn't understand!' "

Emily's words were almost incoherent, but the Earl could see only too clearly what had happened.

What he could not understand was why, after Ophelia's entreaty and his call on her Stepmother this afternoon, this should have happened.

"Have you any idea," he asked, after a pause in which the only sound was Emily's sobs, "why Her Ladyship should have beaten Miss Ophelia tonight, or come to her bedroom to find you giving her some food?"

That, he thought, was the real question he wanted answered—why had Circe decided to beat her stepdaughter before she had any idea that Ophelia was infringing upon the starvation punishment she had imposed upon her.

"It's 'cause Her Ladyship enjoys it, M'Lord," Emily replied. "It's part o' what she an' that French maid gets up to in that wicked place they visit."

"What place?" the Earl asked.

Emily looked uncomfortable.

"P'raps I oughtn't to have said that, M'Lord. I were told not to tell."

"If you want me to help you and Miss Ophelia, you must tell me everything you know," the Earl said. "First of all, who told you not to tell about the place Her Ladyship visits?"

Emily looked uncomfortable again, then she said in a low voice:

" 'Twere J-Jim, M'Lord."

"And who is Jim?" the Earl enquired.

"He's footman on Her Ladyship's carriage. He comes from the country—same as me. I've known him since I were so high."

Emily put out her hand about three feet from the ground.

"What did Jim tell you?" the Earl asked.

"I won't get him into trouble, will I, M'Lord?"

"I promise you Jim will not be in trouble as far as I am concerned," the Earl replied. "But what you know may be of assistance to Miss Ophelia—if you really want to help her."

"I wants to help her—course I do, M'Lord. And if somethin' ain't done quickly, 't might be too late!"

"Then tell me everything you know," the Earl said. "Let us start with Jim."

"Jim drives wi' Her Ladyship."

"And where do they go?"

"To a place in Chelsea, M'Lord, called Limbrick Lane."

"And did Jim tell you what happens there?"

Emily glanced nervously over her shoulder before she said in a voice that the Earl could hardly hear:

" 'Tis magic, M'Lord—wicked, bad magic. They calls on the Devil!"

This was what Lady Harriet had said, the Earl remembered, but he had not believed her.

"And this takes place in a house in Limbrick Lane?"

"Yes, M'Lord."

"How does Jim know that?"

"He goes there so often he's got t' know some of th' neighbours. Terrified they is, he says, of what goes on in Number Thirteen."

"Did they tell him who lives there?"

Again Emily lowered her voice.

"There's an old woman who's called Zenobe or some such name, an' a man who they tells him has been a Parson, but has been . . ."

Emily hesitated for a word.

"Unfrocked?" the Earl suggested.

"I thinks that's it, M'Lord! Seems a funny word to apply to a man—but that's what I thinks Jim said."

"And what else did he say?"

"There's animals taken in there—cocks, an' one day some little goats, bleating terrible they were, one of the women next door tells him—an' none o' them ever came out again!"

The Earl drew in his breath. He had a pretty good idea of what happened at Black Magic ceremonies where there were sacrifices.

"Anything else?" he asked.

"I don't like t' repeat it, M'Lord."

"Nevertheless, I would like to hear it," the Earl insisted. "Remember, Emily, we are concerned only with helping Miss Ophelia."

Emily's voice sank to a whisper.

"Jim says, M'Lord, that he were told th' people in Number Thirteen bought a baby off a woman. Jingling the gold they give her when her left, an' that were never seen again neither!"

The Earl rose to his feet. It was impossible for him to sit listening to any more.

He could hardly credit that what he had heard was the truth, and yet he knew it only substantiated the rumours which had been circulating in the Social World about Circe Langstone.

It was one thing to visit clairvoyants, look into a crystal-ball, or pay for some magic-charms, which he understood quite a lot of women did, but to participate actively in Black Magic ceremonies . . . !

He could understand that such horrors would inflame the desire to inflict cruelty, and for that Ophelia and Rover were conveniently at hand.

"Thank you for speaking so honestly, Emily," he said aloud. "Now tell me, what are you going to do about yourself tonight?"

"I don't know, M'Lord. I asks Her Ladyship that when her said I were to be out o' th' house within an hour.

" 'Where shall I go, M'Lady?' I asked her.

" 'You'll doubtless find a man in th' streets to tell you that,' she answered, ever so nasty. 'And that's the right place, or the river, for you to end up!' "

"But before you left, you went back to see Miss Ophelia?"

"I thinks she were dead, M'Lord, after the punishment she'd taken, but when I speaks to her she says: 'You must go to your father, Emily.'

" 'I can't do that, Miss,' I says. 'I was a-goin' to tell you, but I didn't have th' chance. His Lordship's taken him to the country an' given him a cottage, so I can't join him until there's a Stage-Coach tomorrow morn', an' anyway I've no money.'

" 'Go to the Earl of Rochester, Emily,' Miss Ophelia says in such a weak voice I can hardly hear her. 'I know he will look after you; tell him you are Jem's daughter. Go to him at once! He lives in Berkeley Square, and walk quickly!' "

Emily gave a little sob.

"I wanted to ask if I could help her, M'Lord, but I sees as she were frightened.

" 'Do not stop here talking to me, Emily,' she says. 'Stepmama may come back!' "

Emily looked across the room and finished:

"I just done as she tells me, M'Lord, an' comes here."

"You did exactly the right thing, Emily," the Earl assured her. "I will ask my Housekeeper to look after you tonight, and tomorrow you shall join your father in the country."

"Oh—M'Lord . . . !"

Tears ran down from Emily's eyes as if she had no control over them.

He knew the girl had been terrified that he would not help her and she would have to go back into the streets.

"I am sure I shall be able to find you employment at the Castle," the Earl went on. "Anyway, I will instruct someone to look after you and see what can be done."

"Thank you, M'Lord! Thank you!" Emily cried.

She blew her nose vigorously and wiped her eyes, then she asked:

"Can't you do somethin' for Miss Ophelia, M'Lord? 'Tis not right that she should suffer in such a way."

"No, it is not right," the Earl agreed. "And I promise I will do something to help her."

Emily gave a deep sigh, as if her last anxiety had vanished.

The Earl walked to the fireplace and pulled the bell.

The door opened and the Butler stood there.

"Take Emily to Mrs. Kingstone," he ordered. "She is to stay here tonight and leave for the Castle tomorrow morning. I will speak to Major Musgrove about it."

"Very good, M'Lord."

He looked at Emily and as if he had ordered her to do so she curtseyed, then followed him from the room.

Only when he was alone did the Earl put his hand to his forehead as if to assist his brain to assimilate all he had just heard.

*   *   *

Ophelia fell asleep just before dawn.

It was a sleep of complete exhaustion, so that for a short while she was free of the agonising pain which seared her back like red-hot pokers.

The last thing she heard before she slept was Rover whimpering in pain beneath her bed, and he was still whining when she awoke.

A pale sun was percolating between the curtains, but it was not bright and she guessed that she had in fact been asleep for only an hour or so.

'I cannot move,' she thought, knowing that to do so would send pain like a thousand sharp knives through every nerve in her body.

Then she remembered her promise and knew that somehow she had to reach the Park and see the Earl.

"I cannot get there!" she told herself.

Then as she listened to Rover's whimpering, the idea came to her that if she did meet the Earl she would make him take the dog away.

She knew how perturbed he had been yesterday by

Rover's appearance and she thought that when he saw him today, nothing would stop him from saving the animal that had once belonged to him.

'If she cannot torture Rover, it will be easier to bear my own pain,' Ophelia thought.

Very, very carefully, supporting herself on her hands, she managed to sit up, but it was agony to move, and as she tried to step from the bed onto the floor, she felt that she must faint.

Somehow she managed it, but her breath was coming in quick gasps because of the pain, and her lips were so dry from fear that she felt that they would crack.

She drank a little water, then slowly, so slowly that even to move her arms caused an almost intolerable agony, she dressed herself.

She had the feeling that if she did not leave the house very early she might be prevented from doing so, and it was in fact only quarter-after-six o'clock when she crept down the stairs.

There was really no need to be so secretive. Yet she was afraid, and because her head felt strange and her body ached so intolerably, she could only force herself to think of one thing: that she must save Rover.

The little dog was whimpering and whining and when he tried to walk he could manage it only on three legs.

"I ought to carry you," Ophelia said to him.

But she knew it was difficult enough to move herself without adding the weight of the spaniel.

Somehow they reached the Hall, and it was a relief to find that the door was open because one of the maids in a mob-cap was scrubbing the steps.

She glanced up at Ophelia as she appeared, but she did not speak.

Ophelia knew it was because the whole household had been told that she was in disgrace and they were to have nothing to do with her and not to supply her with anything she might ask for, especially food.

She did not put Rover on a lead. She knew that, like her, he was far too weak to run about, and he only followed her out of affection because she had called him.

Slowly, because it was difficult to put one foot after the other, Ophelia crossed Park Lane, and moved through Stanhope Gate, and went into the Park.

She thought as she reached the grass that the trees were swimming round her and it would be impossible to go any farther.

Then she told herself that she had to get out of sight of the house.

Supposing somebody saw her speaking to the Earl? It was too frightening to think of what would happen to her then.

She forced herself up the small incline to where the trees were close together and the rhododendrons were more in bloom than they had been yesterday.

Then at last, when she felt she would never reach it, there was the seat on which she had sat with the Earl the day before, and as she saw it, she saw him too.

He was there, waiting for her!

The relief of his presence seemed to seep over her, and even as he rose and came walking towards her she felt as if the ground rocked beneath her and suddenly everything went black.

She struggled against it, but it enveloped her like a dark cloud and she knew no more. . . .

* * *

Ophelia stirred, felt a sudden pain shoot across her back, and gave a stifled little cry.

"It is all right," a deep voice said. "You are quite safe. Do not move."

She opened her eyes and saw that the Earl was beside her and his eyes were looking into hers.

Then she was conscious of movement beneath her and somehow she managed to ask:

"Where . . . am . . . I? Wh-what is . . . happening?"

"It is all right," the Earl said again. "I want you to drink this."

As he spoke, he put his hand very gently behind her head and lifted a cup to her lips.

She sipped some liquid and found that it was warm soup, which she swallowed with a little difficulty.

"Try to drink as much as you can," the Earl said. "It will make you feel stronger."

Because she wanted to obey him even though she felt bewildered as to why he was there and why he was feeding her in what she now realised was a moving carriage, she did as he told her.

Only when the cup was half-finished did he say:

"The soup is getting cold. I will refill the cup."

"I . . . do not . . . think I . . . want any . . . more."

"Nonsense!" the Earl replied. "You have to make up for a lot of lost meals, and Rover has eaten so much that he has gone to sleep from sheer gluttony!"

"Rover? He is . . . all right?"

"He is here at your feet," the Earl answered.

Ophelia tried to look at the floor, but it was impossible.

Now she saw that she was in a very comfortable carriage, that she was lying back against a number of satin cushions, and that her legs were covered with a fur rug.

Opposite her, on a small seat of the carriage, she saw her bonnet and realised that the Earl must have removed it while she was unconscious.

"I . . . I am . . . sorry that I . . . f-fainted," she said.

"It is hardly surprising after all you have been through," the Earl replied.

He was busy, she saw, pouring some more soup into the cup from a closed jug which had been kept warm in a hay-basket.

When the cup was half-full he turned back to her.

"Are you strong enough to feed yourself?" he asked.

"Of . . . course," Ophelia replied, "and . . . thank you for being . . . so kind to me."

"You look as if you are in need of kindness," the Earl said quietly.

He did not tell her so, but for one ghastly moment, after she collapsed at his feet, he had thought she was dead.

He had picked her up and carried her to the wooden

seat where they had sat the day before and laid her on
it.

The ashen pallor of her face, the dark lines under
her eyes, and the fact that she seemed emaciated to the
point where everything she wore hung loosely on her,
had really frightened him.

It was only when he had felt her pulse and found it
very faint but beating that he had picked her up again
and carried her through the trees to where his closed
carriage was waiting.

Rover had followed them on three legs without being
told to do so, and it was only when the Earl had placed
Ophelia very carefully inside the carriage that he had
put a cushion on the floor for Rover and laid him, also
very gently, on it.

Jason, who was in attendance, asked:

"Does Your Lordship think his leg's broken?"

"If it is, Henderson will see to it as soon as we reach
the Castle," the Earl replied. "Give the dog something
to eat immediately."

"He looks half-starved, M'Lord!"

"He is!" the Earl said briefly.

As soon as Rover's food had been set down beside
him on the floor of the carriage and he began to eat it
greedily, Jason closed the door and jumped up on the
box, and the coachman had driven off.

The Earl's carriage had been specially built for long
distances and was better sprung than any carriage that
his coach-builders had ever made for anyone else.

With six horses drawing it, as soon as they were
outside the city they moved at a tremendous pace,
sending a billowing cloud of dust up behind them.

The Earl's instructions had been to get to the country as quickly as possible.

He had made his plans very carefully the night before, and what he had decided had of course been
suggested to him by an action of the Restoration
Rochester, who, in 1665, had kidnapped from under
the very nose of another suitor the heiress he wished to
marry.

The difference between that kidnap and the one

planned by the present Earl was that the heiress had
been abducted late at night, when she had left the
Palace of Westminster in her grandfather's coach.

There had been a group of men to carry her into a
coach with six horses and two women to receive her.

The coach had clattered off and was followed by her
abductor—the Earl of Rochester.

This outrageous behaviour had been instrumental in
sending him to the Tower, but the present Earl knew
that the only possible way to save Ophelia was for him
to do the same thing.

John Rochester had, however, kidnapped Elizabeth
Mallet for his own selfish ends, not only because he
loved her but because she was an heiress.

The Earl told himself that *his* action was entirely that
of a philanthropist.

He was not interested in Ophelia as a woman but as
a girl, little more than a child, who was being ill-treated
almost to the point of murder.

Now, as she drank her soup carefully to prevent it
from spilling, he saw the delicacy of her hands, the
bones sharply etched on her thin face, and told himself
that even if he was brought to trial for abduction, his
action was entirely justified.

Not that he had any intention of letting anyone know
that he was involved in the disappearance of Lord Langstone's daughter.

He supposed there would be a hue and cry, but not
at any rate until George Langstone had returned from
Epsom, because he imagined that Circe would in fact
be glad to be rid of Ophelia.

Moreover, there was no reason why she should connect him with her stepdaughter's disappearance, unless
her magic powers gave her a clairvoyant insight that
would not be vouchsafed to any normal being.

Last night he had sat down to write her a letter, to
be delivered this morning.

He regretted, in the most flowery language, that he
was obliged to cancel his invitation for her to dine with
him tonight.

He had written:

For reasons over which I have no control, and I think Your Ladyship can guess what they are, I cannot be at home tonight. I cannot say how much I regret that the dinner we had planned à deux cannot take place. May I give myself the great pleasure of calling on Your Ladyship at the first opportunity to express my apologies and plan another occasion when you will visit my house?

He finished the letter with some fulsome compliments which he knew Circe would appreciate, and ordered Major Musgrove to have it delivered by a groom about noon.

He was quite certain that Circe would imagine he had been ordered to be in attendance on the Prince of Wales.

Like every other woman in London, she would know that His Royal Highness did not like being refused the company of those with whom he wished to surround himself.

He gave Major Musgrove and the rest of his household strict instructions that no-one was to know that he had left London.

Then he ordered his most reliable coachman, upon whose loyalty he could depend as completely as he could upon Jason's, to drive his travelling-coach into the Park.

They were ordered to be waiting from six o'clock onwards at a certain place that the Earl had indicated.

He himself had walked across Park Lane and sat down on the seat which he and Ophelia had occupied the previous day.

As he did so, he wondered what he would do if she failed to appear.

From what Emily had said, there was every likelihood that she would have been too injured to be able to walk and certainly not as far as the seat surrounded by rhododendrons.

But she had come, and that, the Earl told himself, was more important than anything else.

Now, as he took the empty cup from her, he said:

"I have some more food for you, but I think that as you have fasted for so long, you should wait a little."

"It . . . was delicious!" Ophelia said. "And now . . . perhaps . . . I should . . . go home."

"You are not going home."

For a moment his meaning did not seem to penetrate her mind. Then she turned her head sharply, which made her wince, to look at him wide-eyed.

"D-did you . . . say I was not . . . going . . . home?"

"I am taking you away," he said. "Nobody can expect you to stand any more than you have stood already."

"B-but . . . where? What will . . . Stepmama say?"

"She will say nothing that we will hear," the Earl replied, "because she will have no idea where you are."

"But she will . . . wonder what has . . . happened to me."

"I hope it perturbs her," the Earl said drily. "But I think it is your father you should be worried about, rather than your Stepmother."

Ophelia thought this over for a moment, then she said:

"Perhaps she . . . will not tell . . . him."

The Earl looked at her incredulously.

"Are you suggesting that you can disappear without your father knowing of it?"

"He . . . always believes everything Stepmama tells him," Ophelia murmured.

It struck the Earl that it would in fact be quite clever for Circe to tell her husband that his daughter was staying with friends or relations, and therefore she would not have to announce the rather startling news that Ophelia had vanished.

"Did you see anyone this morning before you left the house?"

"Only one of the young housemaids," Ophelia answered. "She was cleaning the front-door steps as I passed her. She did not . . . speak to me because she had been told . . . not to do so."

"How soon will it be before anyone starts worrying when you do not return?"

Ophelia gave him a faint smile.

"No-one . . . I think . . . except for . . . Robinson, the head-housemaid . . . who will have to send somebody else to clean and tidy my bedroom . . . as Emily . . . has been dismissed."

She gave a sudden cry.

"Emily! Did you . . . see her?"

"She is all right," the Earl said soothingly. "She came to me as you told her to do, and I think in an hour or so she too will be leaving for the country to join her father. In the future she will be employed at my Castle."

Impulsively Ophelia put out her hand towards him as she said:

"Thank you . . . thank you. I knew you would help her . . . but I was so afraid . . ."

He knew what she was about to say, and, holding her hand in his warm clasp, he said:

"She reached me without any mishaps. She waited until I returned home and then told me what had happened. I put her in the charge of my Housekeeper."

He saw the tears come into Ophelia's eyes from sheer weakness.

"How . . . can I . . . thank you?"

"By forgetting all you have been through," he answered, "and by becoming strong again and as lovely as you were the first time I saw you."

He saw the surprise in her eyes because he had paid her a compliment, and because he had no wish to embarrass her, he said:

"You should shut your eyes and try to sleep, which I am sure you were unable to do last night. Then when you wake up I will tell you everything else you want to know."

"I am . . . afraid I am . . . dreaming already," Ophelia said. "Are you . . . really taking me . . . somewhere . . . safe?"

"Very, very safe," he replied.

He felt her fingers tighten on his involuntarily, and he said as if he were speaking to a child:

"Do as I tell you and shut your eyes. Then it will be a surprise when you learn where we are going."

Ophelia shut her eyes, and her eye-lashes were dark against her pale cheeks, but now there was a faint smile on her lips.

Still holding her hand as the horses' hoofs thundered over the road, the Earl sat watching her.

Chapter Five

The Earl drove back from the Castle and stopped outside Nanny's small cottage.

He gave the reins to Jason and stepped out of the Phaeton and Nanny met him in the doorway.

"How is she?" the Earl asked.

"I've got her into bed, M'Lord, but who could have treated the young lady in such a terrible fashion?"

There was no doubt of the shocked note in Nanny's voice, and the Earl said:

"How bad is she?"

"Very bad, M'Lord. Her back's raw, and it's shock she'll be suffering! But she's young, and when I've fed her up you'll soon see a difference."

The Earl smiled.

"I know what your 'feeding up' means, Nanny. We shall have to buy her an extra size in gowns."

"That's just what I was a-going to talk to you about, M'Lord."

"I had already thought of it," the Earl said. "I will send you from London everything I think Miss Ophelia needs."

"I've ready for you the gown she's been wearing, M'Lord," Nanny said. "I've washed the blood-stains out and it'll give Your Lordship some idea of her size."

"Thank you, Nanny."

As they were talking they had moved into the little Parlour, and because his head was very near the low ceiling, the Earl sat down on the horse-hair sofa.

"What I am going to suggest, Nanny," he said, "is that you get Emily Bullet, the daughter of a man I have just put into one of these cottages and who is on her way down from London, to give you a hand in looking after Miss Ophelia."

"I've already seen Jem Bullet, M'Lord," Nanny replied. "I remembers him from the old days. He's another that needs feeding up."

"I am sure you will be able to manage that too," the Earl said with a smile. "That reminds me—I have done as you told me and ordered beef-broth and calves'-foot jelly, which the Chef is making at this moment. Mr. Vaughan, the new Agent, will see that you have everything else you require in the way of eggs and chickens."

Nanny gave him a smile which he thought was reminiscent of the days when he had been a particularly good little boy and she was pleased with him.

Then she said briskly:

"And now, M'Lord, I think you should speak to Miss Ophelia before you leave for London. There's something worrying her, but she won't tell me what it is."

"Of course," the Earl agreed.

He rose and climbed the narrow staircase up which he had carried Ophelia an hour or so earlier.

He opened the door of the bedroom which had previously been occupied by Nanny's mother, and saw Ophelia lying back against a number of spotless pillows, her skin almost as white as they were.

At the same time, there was a smile on her lips, which the Earl had not expected.

He walked across the room, noting how fresh and clean everything was, and aware of the scent of lavender, which he was sure came from the linen on the bed.

A small casement window was open under the thatch with which the cottage was roofed, and he could hear the sound of the birds singing outside.

There was a chair by the bed. He sat down on it and asked:

"How are you feeling?"

"I am very . . . grateful to you for . . . bringing me here," Ophelia said, "but I do not want to be a . . . nuisance . . ."

"You will not be that," the Earl replied, "and I can assure you that my old Nanny is delighted to have something to do. She has found time rather heavy on her hands, I think, since she retired from the Castle."

Ophelia did not speak, and after a moment he went on:

"In case you are worrying that it might be too much for her, I am going to tell Jem Bullet to send Emily in every day to help in the cottage as long as you are here."

Ophelia's eyes lit up.

"It will be lovely to have Emily. Your Nanny says I am to stay in bed, which will mean a lot of carrying up and down the . . . stairs."

"Suppose you stop worrying about other people and start thinking about yourself for a change," the Earl suggested.

"What have you . . . done about . . . Rover?"

"I have taken him to my Kennel-man, whose name is Henderson. As Nanny will tell you, he has been at the Castle for many years, and his wife is going to care for Rover as if he were one of her children."

He smiled as he added:

"She has eight, but she tells me there is always room for one more!"

Ophelia smiled, as he had intended, then she said:

"Could . . . anyone be as . . . kind as you have been? B-but I would not . . . wish you to get into any . . . trouble on my . . . account."

As she spoke, the Earl knew that this was what had been perturbing her.

"Trouble?" he questioned lightly.

"I . . . know what people would . . . say if they knew you had . . . brought me here."

"People are going to say nothing," the Earl said firmly, "for no-one will have any idea where you are. This is a very quiet village, and I think you can leave it to Nanny to see that there is not too much gossip amongst those who live in the cottages which belong to me."

There was still an expression of anxiety in Ophelia's eyes, and the Earl bent forward to put his hand over hers as it lay on the white bed-sheet.

"All I want you to think about at the moment," he

said, "is getting well. Then we can discuss your future and find some solution to all your problems."

"You are . . . very . . . very kind," Ophelia said in a low voice, and now there was a suspicion of tears in her eyes.

The Earl rose from the chair.

"I am going back to London," he said, "and I will not be able to come back and see you for some days. If you should want me, or if anything should happen to upset you, Nanny will know how to get in touch with me."

" 'Thank . . . you' is such an . . . inadequate expression," Ophelia murmured, "but you know that both Rover and I are very . . . very grateful."

"As soon as Rover is better he shall come and tell you what he is feeling," the Earl said with a smile.

Then, bending his head under the low lintel, he went from the room.

Ophelia lay back, listening to his footsteps going down the stairs and hearing his deep voice talking with Nanny's high one.

She could not hear what they said, but it gave her a feeling of comfort and of being protected.

How could she have imagined, she thought, this morning when it had been almost impossible to crawl out of bed, that the Earl would have taken charge of her life in such a way that the terror that had overshadowed her like a monstrous cloud had lifted?

For the moment she was no longer afraid.

Downstairs, the Earl gave Nanny quite a number of instructions, then took Ophelia's gown, which had been packed up in a tidy brown-paper parcel, and stepped into his carriage.

But the horses only went a little way down the road to stop outside Jem Bullet's house, and he knew as he saw the little man working in his garden that here was someone else he had made happy.

* * *

Back in London, certain that no-one had noticed his absence of one day, the Earl took up his ordinary life as it had been before Ophelia disrupted it with her question about Jem Bullet.

He escorted the Prince of Wales to the races at Epsom, he attended a Mill on Hampstead Heath, and, because he thought it wise to do so, he spent several evenings with Lady Harriet.

He found himself, and it rather surprised him, being distinctly bored with her conversation when they were not actually making love.

Previously he had always thought that Harriet was different from most of the other women with whom he had affairs, simply because she was prepared to listen to him talking of other subjects besides herself.

But now he thought that much that she said was banal and unimaginative, and only when she discussed Circe Langstone, which she was only too pleased to do, did he become really interested.

"My brother is completely in the doldrums," she said, "and his wife says that he has been so disagreeable at home that she cannot believe he is the same man she married."

"What has that Serpent of Satan done now?" the Earl asked.

Lady Harriet started.

"The Serpent of Satan!" she repeated. "What a good name for her! Why did I not think of that?"

"It is not particularly original," the Earl said, "but that is exactly what she looks like."

"Now that you mention it, of course I see the resemblance," Lady Harriet said. "Oh, Rake, I cannot wait to tell all my friends your most appropriate nickname for her!"

She paused before she said reflectively:

"Most people hate her anyway, and I only wish one of those scurrilous Cartoonists would depict her as a serpent striking at inoffensive men like my darling brother!"

The Earl was rather amused at the idea, and even more so when several men, one after another, came up to him at White's Club and asked if he had heard the latest nickname for Circe Langstone.

He knew that laughter and sarcasm was often a very

effective weapon, which of course had been used to perfection by his namesake.

He remembered some lines John Rochester had written about the Duchess of Cleveland and thought it might almost apply to Circe Langstone:

> *When she has jaded quite*
> *Her almost boundless appetite . . .*
> *She'll still drudge on in tasteless vice*
> *As if she sinn'd for exercise.*

It had, of course, been written when the immoral Duchess was getting old, and he thought the frightening thing was that Circe was a comparatively young woman, no more than twenty-eight or thirty—no-one knew.

But there were certainly a great many years left for her to wreak her evil and go on tormenting other erstwhile faithful husbands like Harriet's brother, or defenseless girls like Ophelia.

Even now the Earl could hardly believe that in what was supposed to be a civilised Society a woman like Circe Langstone could beat anyone so frail as her stepdaughter almost to the point of death.

He was quite certain that if she were able to continue administering such punishments or beatings and starvation, Ophelia could not have survived.

He found himself remembering how, when he had handed Rover over to Henderson, the Kennel-man had said:

"Anyone 'as treats a young dog like this, M'Lord, ought to be exterminated!"

'And that is exactly what ought to happen to Circe Langstone!' the Earl thought to himself.

He was not, however, prepared to act as the Divine Avenger and hang for her murder.

At the same time, because he hated her with the implacable hatred he kept for those who were cruel, the thought of how he could make her suffer for her crimes was permanently in his mind.

He was not surprised to find a letter from her in reply to his.

It was short but full of subtle meaning, and there was no doubt that Circe was waiting eagerly for the invitation he had promised her after having cancelled their dinner together.

The Earl was almost tempted to try making her fall wildly in love with him, as so many other women had done, and then to repudiate her ruthlessly and leave her weeping.

But he had the uncomfortable feeling that Circe was made of sterner stuff. Moreover, everything that was fastidious in him shrank from any point of contact with the woman he loathed.

He knew that Lord Langstone was back in London and he wondered what explanation his wife had given him for the absence of his daughter.

Whatever it might have been, when the Earl saw him sitting in White's, where he too was a Member, he seemed quite unworried and interested in nothing but gaming and drinking.

A week went by and the Earl thought it would cause no comment if it was known that he was visiting his Estate in the country.

Accordingly, choosing a Friday, when even in the Season quite a number of people repaired to their country Estates, if they were near London, he set off, driving himself in his high Phaeton and taking only Jason with him.

He drew up outside the thatched cottage and was conscious of a feeling within himself that was unusual because it was almost one of excitement.

He told himself he simply wanted to see the result of his labours, but, although he was not aware of it, there was something eager in the manner in which he stepped out of his Phaeton and walked up the path to the front door.

He knocked and the door was opened by Emily.

"Oh—M'Lord!" she exclaimed, curtseying, and the Earl smiled at her as he walked in.

He was just about to ask if Miss Ophelia was up-stairs when Nanny came out of the Parlour.

"You couldn't have come on a better day, Master Gerald!" she cried, her face wreathed in smiles. "We've got Miss Ophelia out of bed and downstairs for the first time, and now you can have a cup o' tea with her!"

"I would like to do that," the Earl answered, and walked into the Parlour.

Ophelia was sitting in an arm-chair by the table, which was laden with all the delicacies that he remembered enjoying in his boyhood.

When she saw who was there, she gave a little cry of sheer delight.

"How lovely to see you! I am so glad I am downstairs and no longer an invalid."

The Earl sat down beside her, realising, as the door shut behind him, that Nanny had tactfully left them alone.

"You look better!"

As he spoke, he thought that this was an understatement.

She looked entirely different from the thin, white-faced creature who had seemed almost on the point of death when he had carried her up the stairs a week ago.

Now there was colour in Ophelia's cheeks and she had undoubtedly put on a little weight, but what made all the difference, the Earl thought, was that for the first time since he had known her, she looked happy.

"I am so glad you have come," she said, "because I have been wanting to thank you, but Nanny would not let me write to you."

"I do not wish to be thanked."

"But I have to!" Ophelia insisted. "For those beautiful ... gowns you sent me and ... all the other ... things as well."

She looked a little shy and the Earl knew she was referring to the nightgowns and lace-trimmed chemises that he had ordered from a shop in Bond Street which he had patronised for a long time.

It was not only his official mistresses who expected him to pay for the things he admired, but even Ladies of Quality like Lady Harriet were delighted to accept gowns and other garments that they always said were too expensive for their own purses.

He got very cynical about the way they extracted payment for their favours in exactly the same manner as a prostitute did, but with the refinement of providing a bill.

Their pretences also irritated him.

Only last week Harriet had appeared in a very expensive velvet cape trimmed with ermine when he took her to Covent Garden.

"Do you like it?" she had asked, twisting round so he could inspect her from every angle.

"Like what?"

"My cape!"

"Very pretty."

"I thought you would think so, Rake darling, but I've only borrowed it. It is too expensive for my little purse, so I must return it tomorrow."

It had been easier to say: "Send the bill to me," than to have her sulking all through the evening!

The Earl took his eyes from Ophelia's face to see that she was wearing a very pretty dress of white muslin sprigged with coloured flowers.

It made her look very young, the personification of spring, and he thought she matched the big bowl of narcissus which stood in the centre of the table.

"I never thought . . . I should ever own such beautiful clothes," she said, "but . . . how can I pay you back?"

"They are a present," the Earl said.

She looked at him a little shyly, then said:

"You know it is . . . incorrect for a . . . gentleman to give a lady . . . articles of . . . clothing."

It was, the Earl thought, a rule which worried few women of his acquaintance, but he replied:

"I think what is conventional for a number of people, Ophelia, hardly applies to us. We have in fact been unconventional ever since we met."

"That is . . . true," Ophelia agreed, "but I feel . . . embarrassed at . . . costing you so much . . . money."

"I can afford it!" the Earl replied lightly. "And you could hardly have stayed with Nanny with nothing to wear but her nightgowns, which I am sure are thick, sensible, and definitely Puritanical."

Ophelia gave a little laugh.

"They are just like my own Nanny's," she said, "very, very concealing, like a tent."

They both laughed, and the Earl thought Ophelia's laughter was something he had always wanted to hear, although he had not been aware of it.

"And now you are downstairs for the first time," he said, looking at the loaded table.

There were muffins and rock-cakes, the inevitable Madeira-cake which he remembered from when he had been in the Nursery, besides sponges and, what he knew was a special treat, jam-cornets.

Ophelia saw where he was looking and said in a whisper:

"I do hope you will stay and help me eat some of this. Nanny will be so hurt if it is not all finished up, and I find it impossible to eat even half of what she cooks for me."

"You will have to do what she tells you," the Earl said. "I have always had to do so!"

"I do not think that is quite true," Ophelia replied. "Nanny tells me you were very naughty and very self-willed."

"Nonsense!" the Earl said firmly. "I was a model child in every way!"

His eyes were twinkling and Ophelia said:

"Nanny thinks that the sun and the moon rise on you alone and the world revolves round you. At the same time, she disapproves of quite a number of the . . . things you . . . do."

"Then I can only hope she has not been telling you about them," the Earl said.

"I like hearing about you," Ophelia replied. "It makes everybody else's life, especially mine, seem very dull."

"That is the last word I should have applied to your life so far," the Earl said drily, "and I would have chosen the word 'dramatic' rather than 'dull.' "

He realised that Ophelia had spoken without thinking, and now when she knew he was referring to the manner in which her Stepmother had treated her, the colour rose in her face.

As if what he had said brought back memories she was trying to forget, she asked in a low voice:

"Have you ... heard ... anything?"

"Nothing," the Earl replied. "I have seen your father in White's, but I have not spoken to him, and thankfully I have not set eyes on your Stepmother since I last saw you."

"That must ... make her very ... angry!"

There was no doubt about the fear that was back in Ophelia's voice, and the Earl said quickly:

"Even if it does, there is no need for it to perturb you. You just have to forget her and realise that you are starting a new life altogether."

"A ... very different ... life," Ophelia said. "Everybody is ... so kind ... it is almost like being ... at home ... with Mama."

There was something wistful in the way she spoke which told the Earl how much she missed her mother.

"You still have to do what I told you when I brought you here," the Earl said. "Get well, and do not worry about anything except that."

"We shall have to ... talk about it ... sometime," Ophelia said.

"Of course," the Earl agreed, "but not now. Not on what is a very auspicious occasion, when you have come downstairs for the first time!"

He looked again at the table, then said:

"Much as the idea of eating many of those extremely fattening cakes appeals to me, I think I had better call Nanny and get it over."

He spoke in a tone which made Ophelia laugh. Then she said:

"Before she comes in ... there is ... something I want to ... say to you."

There was a note in her voice which told the Earl that she was very serious.

"What is it?" he asked gently.

Ophelia paused for a moment, then she said:

"Do you think that magic ... Black Magic ... can reach one ... however carefully one ... hides from it?"

The Earl was still.

He was aware that she was worried.

"Tell me what is troubling you."

"E-Emily tells me that ... Stepmama practises ... Black Magic," Ophelia said. "I ... f-find it hard to ... believe ... but there are ... things that are ... frightening."

"What sort of things?"

"Sometimes at night," Ophelia answered, "I can ... see her f-face quite clearly ... not only in my mind ... but when I open my ... eyes she is ... there ... in the darkness!"

There was a tremulous note in her voice which made the Earl feel apprehensive, then he said:

"I am sure it is just imagination."

"That is ... what I tell myself," Ophelia answered. "At the same ... time, her ... eyes seem to be ... looking at me ... compelling me ... drawing me!"

She made a little gesture with her hands.

"It is ... difficult to explain ... and yet ... when it is there it is ... very real."

The Earl found himself remembering how in India the Fakirs, and the other people with whom he had talked, believed strongly in thought-transference. The natives always knew what was going to happen long before it occurred.

He had found himself puzzled and intrigued hundreds of times by what he thought was a kind of clairvoyance or quite simply the transference of thought from one person to another.

If Circe was practising Black Magic then perhaps she could get in touch with her stepdaughter wherever she might be hiding.

He did not wish to suggest any of these ideas to Ophelia because he thought it would only make her more worried than she was already. Instead he asked:

"What do you do when you see your Stepmother's face?"

"I pray," Ophelia replied simply. "I pray very hard ... but somehow it is not ... enough ... I can feel ..."

She paused and the Earl said:

"Go on! I want to hear."

"You will think I am very . . . foolish," she said, "but I can . . . feel her reaching out towards me . . . like some horrible . . . insidious . . . evil!"

As she spoke, without, the Earl realised, being aware of what she was doing, she slipped her hand into his.

"Please . . . help me," she whispered. "I am . . . frightened!"

The Earl thought to himself that she had every reason to be, and as he held her fingers, which were trembling in his strong clasp, he said:

"I will tell you what I will do—I will bring from the Castle a picture which was given to me by someone who wished to express her gratitude."

"As I . . . do."

"Exactly!" the Earl agreed. "And like you, she thought I had saved her life."

"Was it one of the people you rescued during the French Revolution?" Ophelia asked.

"Who told you about that?"

"Nanny told me how incredibly brave you were and how you not only helped the emigrés to escape but supported them when they arrived in London, absolutely penniless."

As she spoke, there was a look of admiration in Ophelia's eyes which the Earl could not mistake.

"I was very lucky," he said, "not only to bring some of the French men and women out alive, but also myself."

"And if you had been . . . killed," Ophelia said, "then you would not have been able to . . . help me."

"Exactly!" the Earl agreed, "but I am here, and therefore I intend to help you, Ophelia. You have to believe me when I tell you that the picture I will bring you will protect you from your Stepmother because its power of good is much stronger than hers of evil."

"Oh . . . please . . ." Ophelia said, "may I have it soon . . . today?"

"I will fetch it as soon as I have had my tea," the Earl promised, "but you know as well as I do that we must not upset Nanny."

"No . . . of course not," she agreed.

The Earl rose to his feet to call Nanny into the room.

But while he joked and smiled as they ate their tea, his thoughts were on Circe Langstone.

For the first time he was beginning to take her interest in Black Magic really seriously.

Previously he had thought of her merely as a cruel, extremely unpleasant woman with a sadistic impulse to inflict suffering.

Now, because of what Ophelia had told him, he had begun to believe that it was even more serious than that.

Only because of his experiences in India did he not laugh at the talk of magic, as any of his contemporaries would have done.

He had seen the Fakirs perform supernatural acts which could not be attributed to hypnotism nor to the credulity of those who watched them.

Because he had been interested in the Indians, as a great number of Englishmen were not, he had found many doors open to him that were closed to other white men.

He had had the privilege of meeting Saddhus who were undoubtedly as holy as their followers believed.

On his return to England the Earl had not kept up this interest in the occult.

But now everything he had read and discovered came back to him and he knew that if in fact Circe was indulging in Black Magic practises, they might be more powerful than any ordinary person would credit.

It would have been easy to laugh at what could have been a sick girl's fantasies and believe that her Stepmother had terrorised her to the point where even to think of her might cause her face to materialise in front of her.

But the Earl felt uncomfortably that it was more than that, something which he could not explain but was not prepared to dismiss as impossible.

When he reached the Castle he went first to the kennels to see how Rover was faring.

Like Ophelia, the dog looked quite different, and his leg, which fortunately had suffered only a simple fracture, was, Mrs. Henderson told him, almost healed.

He was fatter and not so nervous, but when the Earl suggested that Rover was now well enough to be with Ophelia, Mrs. Henderson begged that he might stay for another week.

The Earl gave in to her request good-humouredly, then went into the Castle to find the picture he had promised Ophelia.

It had in fact been given to him by the Marquise de Valmont after he had brought her, her husband, and their children to safety from France, disguised so cleverly that although they went through hair-raising experiences, no-one ever suspected that their names were on the list for the guillotine.

The Earl remembered the terrible journey back to England in a small fishing-boat. There had been a storm which had made him fear that at the last moment, after all they had been through, they would never reach safety.

But finally they had arrived, and when he had called on *Madame* de Valmont two days later in London, he had been very touched when she made him a gift of the picture.

"It has been in my family for hundreds of years," she said, "and is supposed to contain a small piece of the veil of Saint Veronica, who, if you remember, wiped the forehead of Christ when He was on His way to His crucifixion."

She gave him a charming smile as she said:

"That may not be actually true, but at the same time, because of the faith of those who have revered this small picture, which for centuries stood in the Chapel in my father's Château, there are a large number of miracles attributed to it."

"I must not take it from you," the Earl said quickly.

"It is the most precious thing I possess," the Marquise said, "with the exception of my husband and my children, and as you have given me these I can only ask you to accept this, because I give it to you from my heart."

The Earl felt he could not refuse in such circumstances, but as the De Valmonts remained close friends, he was always determined that one day he would return

the small picture, which was little larger than a minia-
ture, to their children.

Now as he picked it up in its beautifully chased gold
frame, he looked at the face of Saint Veronica painted
by a skilled artist and at the small piece of real linen
which she held in her pictured hands.

'This will help Ophelia,' he thought, and was surprised how firmly he believed that this was possible.

He thought, with a slightly mocking smile, that
Ophelia had not only encroached on his life but also
in some strange way had altered his attitude towards it.

A month ago he would have scoffed at the idea of his
finding something holy to combat the forces of evil, and
yet that was what he was doing, with a sincerity which
amounted to a faith which he did not know he possessed.

As he felt slightly uncomfortable at his own thoughts,
he wrapped the picture in his clean linen handkerchief
and put it in his pocket.

Then he interviewed his new Agent and learnt of all
the things that had been altered on the Estate since he
had sacked Aslett.

"I'm afraid, M'Lord," Mr. Vaughan said, "that there
are many discrepancies in the farm accounts, and every
day I keep finding new ways in which money has been
drained off the Estate illegally."

"Attend first to the people who have suffered," the
Earl ordered. "Are the farmers quite happy now?"

"Very happy indeed, M'Lord, thanks to your generosity," Mr. Vaughan replied. "But there are certain im-
provements to many of the farm buildings which I
would like to discuss with Your Lordship."

"I will try to come down again next week," the Earl
promised, "and we will go into every detail."

"Thank you very much indeed, M'Lord."

Mr. Vaughan spoke almost as if his employer had
given him a present.

The Earl liked the enthusiasm of the man he had
appointed, who was younger and less experienced than
might have been expected of the Agent on such a large
and important Estate.

But Vaughan had been recommended by Major
Musgrove, and he was another soldier who had been

discarded by an ungrateful Government which was
turning a deaf ear to the martial sounds on the other
side of the Channel.

The Earl drove back to the village, but when he
entered the cottage Nanny said to him:

"I've put Miss Ophelia to bed, M'Lord. She's had
enough—although she won't admit it, and wanted to
wait for your return."

"I hope you will still allow me to see her, Nanny,"
the Earl said with a twinkle in his eye.

"You knows as well as I do, M'Lord, that your Lady
Mother would not have approved of your going upstairs."

"My 'Lady Mother,' as you call her, is fortunately
not here to reprimand us," the Earl replied, "and
therefore you must just turn a blind eye to my unconventional behaviour."

"It's something I've done often enough, M'Lord,"
Nanny said sharply.

"And will go on doing!" the Earl said with a smile.
"By the way, you have indeed done a good job on Miss
Ophelia. I can hardly believe she is the same girl!"

"She's certainly better in health and spirits," Nanny
answered, "and a nicer, sweeter young lady it's never
been my pleasure to meet. Anyone who could treat her
in such a manner must be a fiend, and there's no other
word for it."

"You have hit the nail on the head!" the Earl exclaimed. "That is exactly what Her Ladyship is—a
fiend!"

He was well aware as he climbed the staircase that
Emily would have related to Nanny every detail about
Circe, so there was no point in pretending that it was
not Ophelia's Stepmother who had treated her with such
bestiality.

He entered the small bedroom and Ophelia gave a
little cry of delight.

"I am so glad you've come to see me!" she exclaimed.
"Nanny insisted on sending me to bed and I was afraid
that you would go back to London without saying
good-bye."

"I made you a promise to bring you something," the Earl answered, "and you should know by this time that I never break my promises."

She smiled at him and her eyes were excited as he drew the picture from his pocket and she undid the handkerchief.

She looked at it for a moment or two before she said: "I think it is Saint Veronica!"

"That is clever of you," the Earl said, "and she is holding what is believed to be an actual piece of her veil."

Ophelia looked down at the picture, then raised her eyes to the Earl's.

"I can feel the . . . holiness about this," she said. "How can I thank you for lending it to me?"

"It will keep you safe," the Earl said, with a positiveness that surprised him. "Put it near your bed, and when you are frightened by apparitions of any sort, hold it in your hands and say your prayers as you told me you have been doing."

"I will," she answered, "and perhaps . . ."

She hesitated.

"Perhaps?" the Earl questioned.

"Perhaps, because you are . . . so strong and so . . . kind, you will . . . pray for me too?"

The Earl looked at her in astonishment.

He had been asked to do many things in his life by beautiful women but no-one had ever asked that he should pray for them.

"I doubt if my prayers will be heard," he answered, after a moment's pause.

"They will," Ophelia said, "because you hate . . . cruelty and are . . . very, very brave."

"I think you have a rather biased view of my character," the Earl said. "You must not believe everything Nanny tells you."

"She loves you," Ophelia said, "and I cannot imagine that any man could have had a more fascinating and exciting history. It is like listening to the stories of heroes that I read when I was at School."

The Earl put up his hands in mock horror.

"Now you are frightening me!" he said. "I am going straight back to London, because I refuse to be made a hero or a saint or anything except what I am."

"What is that?" Ophelia asked curiously.

"You know my nickname," he answered. "A Rake! A cynic! And those who listen to me in the House of Lords will tell you that I am also a satirist."

"That too sounds rather exciting," Ophelia answered, "but it is only one part of your character, as you well know."

"Now you are canonising me again," the Earl said, "so I will leave you, Ophelia, and please go on doing exactly what Nanny tells you, so that you will look even better than you do at this moment."

She stretched out her hand to him. As he raised it to his lips he realised that her fingers clung to his as if she could not bear to let him go.

"You will . . . come again . . . soon?" she asked wistfully.

"Very soon," he replied.

Then as she sat up in bed against her pillows, holding the picture of Saint Veronica in her hands, he smiled at her and left.

* * *

As he drove back to London the Earl found himself thinking of Circe Langstone and wondering how her nefarious excursions into the Black Arts could be prevented.

He had rather doubted the story that Emily had told him of a baby being taken into the house in Limbrick Lane and never seen again.

But now he had to admit to himself that it was quite a possibility.

Babies were a very important part of Black Magic ceremonies and so-called witches used their brains and their blood in various ways.

It seemed incredible that, when they were no longer living in the Middle Ages, a Temple where Satan was worshipped should be operating in a London suburb.

Yet the stories that Jim had related to Emily seemed to be too factual to be ignored.

The unfrocked Priest, the cocks and goats going into the house never to be seen again, the baby, and now Ophelia seeing the materialisation of Circe's face and compelling eyes.

It was all such a familiar pattern that the Earl found it difficult to laugh it away as a product of imagination.

Even if the neighbours of No. 13 Limbrick Lane were just naturally curious about what was taking place, if it was nothing out of the ordinary, why was someone of Lady Langstone's social standing visiting such a place?—and not once but continually?

Fashionable fortune-tellers, and there were dozens of them, were usually brought to the house of a Lady of Quality, and then, having been rewarded with money and a meal, were sent away again.

That Circe herself should go anywhere as squalid as Limbrick Lane was extremely significant.

It meant, the Earl conjectured, that the stories of the animals to be sacrificed were probably true.

The question was, what could he do about it?

Black Magic was, of course, forbidden by law in the Witchcraft Act, but a case against those perpetrating it would evoke a considerable amount of publicity and that would involve Lord Langstone and perhaps Ophelia as well.

The more he thought of it, the more difficult he found it to discover a way in which he could stop Circe Langstone not only from indulging in Black Magic practises, but also from frightening her stepdaughter with them.

He wondered if any good could be done if he faced her with the fact that he knew a great deal more than she would wish him to know.

Then he told himself that that would undoubtedly reveal where Ophelia was hidden and ruin her reputation.

No-one in the Social World would believe for one moment, that he had abducted her out of sheer pity.

They would be quite certain that she was his mistress, and in that case she would be ostracised completely by everybody of consequence in the *Beau Monde*.

"What the devil can I do?" the Earl asked himself, as he had asked before, and once again he felt as though he was up against a brick wall.

Then an idea came to him and for a moment it seemed so outrageous that he merely laughed at himself.

Nevertheless, it persisted, and he remembered how his namesake had disguised himself as a porter or a beggar to mix with drunkards and thieves and once had deceived the citizens of Burford into thinking him a tinker.

Crying, "Pots and pans to mend!" in the market-place, he had waited until a large collection of them lay heaped round him, and had then proceeded to knock their bottoms out or hammer them into grotesque shapes.

He was not recognised, but the tradition in Burford was that His Lordship afterwards sent new pots and pans to all concerned.

There was nothing new in such pranks even in the reign of Charles II.

Plutarch recorded that Mark Antony would go up and down the city disguised as a slave, and Cleopatra often accompanied him, dressed like a chambermaid.

The Earl also remembered how often he had used disguises of every sort in France and how many people he had helped escape by this means.

There was a room in Berkeley Square where the clothes he had used were still kept and to which only he had the key.

He would go and see for himself, he thought, what was going on at No. 13 Limbrick Lane.

Then he would learn whether the stories he had listened to were exaggerated or whether they were based on fact.

He turned the idea over and over in his mind, but when he reached London he was still undecided and had not come to a certain conclusion.

Only later that night, when he was once again thinking of Circe Langstone, he told himself that if his name for her, the "Serpent of Satan," was appropriate, it was important to remember that snakes were dangerous.

Then he recalled an incident which had occurred when he was young.

He had been out shooting with one of his father's Keepers and they had found a nest of rats in the farm-yard. They killed one rat but the others ran into a disused drainpipe which was lying on the ground.

"What can we do now?" the Earl had asked.

"We'll smoke 'em out, Master Gerald," the Keeper had replied.

He had twisted some straw together and stuffed it down one end of the pipe, then set it alight.

One by one the rats came running out at the other end, and the Earl shot them.

It would be impossible to shoot Circe, he thought as he lay awake in the darkness, much as he would like to do so. But what had happened to the rats kept re-curring in his mind.

In the morning, caution told him that he must behave normally and give no grounds for anyone to suspect for one moment that he had anything to do with Ophelia's disappearance.

Despite the fact that his brain told him that any sensible man would be sceptical of all things which were called supernatural, he found it hard to believe that Ophelia was not experiencing something undoubtedly abnormal.

With any other woman he would have put down what she told him first to imagination, and secondly to a desire to attract and hold his attention.

This, he knew, was an idea utterly without foun-dation with regard to Ophelia, and no woman in such circumstances could have behaved more quietly and without any sign of hysteria.

The Earl remembered one lady he had favoured who had been held up and robbed by footpads.

They had taken nothing but her jewels, but for weeks she had wept to evoke his sympathy and swooned if the coach in which they were driving had to slow down in traffic.

She had over-dramatised what had occurred until the Earl became so bored with the repetition of her fears that he dropped her.

Ophelia had behaved with a commendable courage and a self-control that many men might have envied.

"She is a very exceptional person," the Earl told himself, and was more determined than ever that he would make Circe relinquish her hold over her stepdaughter.

The question was, how?

How?

Chapter Six

The Earl, riding home through the Park, deep in his thoughts, heard a voice call: "Rake!" and turned his head to find that a friend had ridden up beside him.

"Hello, Henry!" he exclaimed. "I have not seen you for a long time."

"I have been in France," Henry Carlton replied.

"Paying your respects to the First Consul?" the Earl enquired.

"I met him, and he is certainly very genial," Henry Carlton replied, "but I do not need to tell you that the ship-yards and the munitions-factories are working day and night."

"That is what I heard," the Earl said grimly.

"Well, I hope you will shout it loud and long in the ears of our deaf Ministers," Henry Carlton said, "and I will tell you something else, Rake—Napoleon intends to crown himself Emperor!"

The Earl looked surprised.

"Do you really mean that?"

"It will only be fulfilling the prophecies of his astrologers and fortune-tellers, to whom he has listened for years."

"Good heavens!" the Earl exclaimed. "Are you really telling me that Napoleon of all people goes in for that type of nonsense?"

"He does indeed," Henry Carlton replied, "and so does his wife, Josephine. Of course, every prediction is more favourable than the last."

"That goes without saying," the Earl replied cynically, "but I can hardly credit that someone as astute and undoubtedly brilliant in many ways as Bonaparte would be influenced by such trickery."

"It is very much in the French tradition," his friend

113

replied. "*Madame* de Mantenon practised Black Magic to gain the attention of Louis XIV, and Catherine de Medici went in for the whole caboodle—sacrifices and of course the Black Mass said over the body of a virgin."

"I dislike everything about it!" the Earl exclaimed violently.

"I agree with you," Henry Carlton agreed, "but be ready to see the little Corsican Corporal amongst the Crowned Heads of Europe!"

They parted as they reached Stanhope Gate and the Earl rode home thinking of what his friend had told him.

He knew it would be a shock for the majority of Parliamentarians that Napoleon should aspire to a Monarchy, but he told himself that it was in fact something that might have been expected from a man who had flamed like a meteor over the map of Europe.

Breakfast was waiting for the Earl, and as soon as he had finished, Major Musgrove came in with the correspondence that had to be attended to and a great number of questions concerning the Earl's other Estates.

It took them until nearly eleven o'clock to get through all that had to be done.

Finally, when the Earl had signed the last letter, he rose to his feet and said:

"I must change. I have promised to be at Carlton House at noon."

"I am sorry to have kept you so long, My Lord," Major Musgrove said.

"I do not think we have wasted our time on anything that was unnecessary," the Earl replied with a smile.

He was just about to leave the Library when the Butler came in with a note on a silver salver.

"A groom has just arrived with this, M'Lord, from the Castle!"

The Earl opened the envelope, and as soon as he saw the hand-writing on the letter inside, he realised that it was from Nanny.

She had obviously scrawled it in a hurry for the script was not as neat or precise as he remembered.

He read:

My Lord,
  I would be greatly obliged if Your Lordship would visit us as soon as possible. There are things going on which I don't like and don't understand, and I think Your Lordship should come.
                              I remain,
                              Your Respectful Servant,
                              Nanny

The Earl read the letter carefully, then said to the Butler, who was waiting for his instructions:

"Tell the groom from the Castle that there will be no answer for him to carry on his return, and order my Phaeton with four horses and Jason to come round immediately!"

"Very good, M'Lord."

The Earl looked at his Comptroller.

"Send a message to Carlton House to inform the Prince of Wales that I have been unavoidably called to the country on family affairs, and express my deep regret at not being able to attend on His Royal Highness as I promised to do."

"Very good, My Lord," Major Musgrove said. "Also, you have arranged to visit the Lady Harriet this afternoon."

"Send my deep apologies to Her Ladyship too," the Earl said over his shoulder, for by this time he was halfway across the Hall.

He had changed and was downstairs a few minutes after the Phaeton had been brought round from the stables.

He stepped into it and drove off, and was almost clear of the London traffic before half-after-eleven.

As he went, he was wondering what could have upset Nanny, for he knew that she would not have sent for him unless it had been really urgent.

It seemed impossible that Circe Langstone might

have discovered the whereabouts of her stepdaughter, but if she had, surely the obvious course for her to have taken would be to demand that Ophelia should return home immediately.

If that had happened, Nanny would have told him about it in her letter, so it was therefore something else, something different, which was upsetting her.

The Earl was seldom talkative when he was driving and today he made no effort to speak to Jason on the two-hour journey.

Other people with not such good horse-flesh and with heavier vehicles took longer, but the Earl prided himself that he could reach Rochester Castle in a hundred and twenty minutes, and no-one to date had broken his record.

He wondered if the groom would get there before him to tell Nanny that he was on his way, but he thought that was unlikely, even though it was obviously quicker to travel on horse-back and across country.

But he was certain that the man, having arrived in London, would take a rest in the Servants' Hall and doubtless be provided with a good meal and a glass of ale before he set off on his return journey.

He hoped that the groom would not be too talkative, but even if he did say there was a young girl staying with Nanny Graham, whom many of the older servants would remember, there was no reason why they should connect her with Lord and Lady Langstone's daughter.

He had in fact told Nanny to be careful not to let anyone in the village know Ophelia's surname.

Only Emily would be aware of her true identity, and what he had seen of Jem Bullet's daughter told him that she could be trusted.

The Earl thought he had planned everything with his usual efficiency and eye for detail. It was something on which he prided himself and for which he had gained quite a reputation when he was with his Regiment.

However, despite his regular conviction that few things perturbed or ruffled his peace of mind, he was relieved when he had his first sight of the village and its row of black and white thatched cottages.

He drew up outside Nanny's cottage, his Phaeton's wheels leaving a cloud of dust behind them.

Even as he stepped out, the door was opened and Nanny stood there.

One glance at her face, even before he reached her, told the Earl that something was very much amiss.

"Oh, Master Gerald!" she exclaimed as usual, forgetting, when she was shaken out of the commonplace, to address him formally. "Thank God you've come! I've been praying you wouldn't be too long."

It was obvious from her attitude that something had gone very wrong, and the Earl thought it wise to close the front door behind him before he spoke. When he had done so, he asked:

"What is the matter, Nanny"

"They've taken her, M'Lord. It's what I was afraid of when I wrote to you."

"They?" the Earl questioned. "Who are 'they'? What has happened?"

Nanny drew in her breath and he saw that her hands were trembling.

"Sit down, Nanny," he said gently, "and tell me what has occurred."

Nanny sat down as if her legs would not carry her, and because he felt that she needed reassuring, the Earl sat too.

"Start at the beginning," he said. "Why did you write to me?"

"It was because there was a man snooping about the village," Nanny replied, "asking questions. I even caught him peeping in through my windows!"

"What sort of man?"

"A nasty-looking fellow," Nanny answered. "Not a labouring man, if you understands my meaning, M'Lord, and certainly not a gentleman!"

"Go on," the Earl prompted.

"I didn't like the look of him and I fancied it would frighten Miss Ophelia if she knew what was happening."

"You did not tell her?" the Earl enquired.

"No, I didn't tell her," Nanny replied. "She's been so much better and happier these last few days, and she's slept like a child with your picture in her hands."

"So you saw this man, and you wrote to me," the Earl continued, "and as you see, I have come in answer to your letter."

"It's too late, M'Lord! Too late!" Nanny wailed, and tears came into her eyes.

"Miss Ophelia has been taken away?" the Earl questioned.

"Yes, M'Lord, about an hour ago. I sent Emily up to the Castle to fetch Mr. Vaughan, but she hasn't come back yet."

"What happened?" the Earl asked.

"I was baking a cake in the kitchen, M'Lord," Nanny explained, "and Miss Ophelia was helping me. She said she wanted to learn to cook like I do, and we were both standing at the table, laughing about something she'd said, when suddenly the door bursts open!"

"You did not hear a carriage arriving?" the Earl asked.

"I suppose we should have, if we'd been listening for one," Nanny answered, "'cause when they seized her, there was a carriage outside and the door was open."

"Who seized her?"

"The man I'd seen peeping through the window, and another. Strange-looking he was."

"In what way?"

"He appeared to be wearing a kind of cassock," Nanny said, "but he didn't have the Parson's bands at the neck, if you get my meaning. It might have been just a long black coat."

The Earl thought she was right in thinking that it was a cassock, and now he knew what had happened.

"They took hold of Miss Ophelia as she was standing there, and without saying a word!" Nanny said.

"What did she do?" the Earl asked.

"She gave a little cry of surprise, then asks: 'What do you want? Who are you?' But before she could say any more, they dragged her out of the house and down through the garden and bundled her into the carriage."

She paused.

"I heard her scream, then the carriage drove off and

I couldn't hear anything more. Oh, M'Lord, it was horrible!"

Nanny's voice broke and the tears began to run down her cheeks.

The Earl put out his hand and laid it over hers.

"I am sure it was, Nanny," he said, "but do not worry. I will bring her back to you."

"You know where she's been taken?" Nanny questioned.

"I have a good idea," the Earl replied. "Just tell me how many men there were on the box of the carriage."

Nanny thought for a moment.

"Only one, M'Lord," she said through her tears.

"And how many horses?"

"Two, M'Lord."

"Thank you, Nanny."

The Earl went out of the cottage and swung himself back into the Phaeton.

He had to move his horses a little way down the road before he could turn them. Then he started back the way they had come, at a pace which made Jason stare at him in surprise.

They had driven a long way and the Earl was congratulating himself that despite the double journey his horses were standing up well to the extra exertion he was putting on them, before he said in a quiet voice:

"The young lady we took to Nanny Graham, Jason, has been abducted!"

"Abducted, M'Lord?"

"Yes, Jason, and there are three men with her, but I think we can manage them."

"I'm sure we can, M'Lord."

"Are we carrying a pistol with us?"

"Yes, M'Lord. It's under the seat."

It was usual in all the Earl's carriages to carry a pistol in case they were held up by highwaymen.

It was something that had actually never happened, but the Earl believed in taking precautions against every eventuality.

Many of his friends had been robbed when travelling the countryside or late at night in London by footpads or mounted highwaymen against whom they had no defense.

Jason bent to bring from its hiding-place under the seat the pistol that was primed and loaded.

"Better check it carefully," the Earl said. "It has not been used recently."

"I checked it, M'Lord, about a month ago," Jason replied.

"Then it will prove effective if necessary."

"Does Your Lordship think that them who have taken the young lady'll be armed?"

"I have no idea," the Earl replied, "but I would not put murder past them if it suited them!"

He drove on and his expression was grim.

He knew only too well why Ophelia had been abducted by those who lived at No. 13 Limbrick Lane.

Even before Henry Carlton had spoken of the Black Mass which was said over the body of a virgin, it had crossed his mind that if those who worshipped Satan were prepared to sacrifice a child, they would certainly not flinch from the most important of all Black Magic ceremonies.

This was the Mass said backwards in front of an inverted cross over the naked body of a pure girl.

The Earl knew that at the end of such ceremonies the victim either died from her injuries or went mad from the horrors in which she had been forced to participate.

The idea of anything so horrible happening to Ophelia made him know that he would not hesitate to kill any man who tried to prevent him from rescuing her.

"I have to save her!" he said beneath his breath.

Now he was fighting not only a crusade against cruelty, which he abhorred, but also because he himself was personally involved.

He knew, as he drove in a manner which extracted from his team every ounce of their strength and sent a huge cloud of dust billowing out over the countryside as they thundered over the dry roads, that what he felt for Ophelia was different from anything he had ever felt before.

Her frailty, her weakness, and her child-like trust in him had made him vulnerable in a manner which he had never suspected was possible.

Always in the past the women who had amused and excited him had met him on an equal footing and there had been between them a fiery desire that was entirely physical, easily aroused, and as far as he was concerned just as easily quenched.

He thought now that astonishingly, almost incredibly, in the short time he had known Ophelia, she had crept into his heart.

From the moment he had first seen her, she had intrigued him as no woman had ever done before, and he had found it impossible to forget her.

He had told himself glibly that it was only because she had upset him by accusing him of neglecting Jem Bullet, but he was honest enough to admit that it was much more than that.

Her little face with its huge, frightened eyes had haunted him, and now he knew why he had found Lady Harriet banal and rather dull.

There was something about Ophelia that had stimulated his mind and aroused in him new ideas that had not been there before.

It was not what she said, it was what she *was,* and that, he told himself with a faintly mocking smile, was inescapable.

On they went, the horses striving their utmost to do what was required of them, and seeming to eat up the long miles which led back towards London.

Then when the Earl was wondering, almost despairingly, if the carriage he sought had perhaps taken another route, he saw it just ahead, rising up a small incline with trees on either side.

"I think that is the carriage we are seeking, Jason!" he exclaimed.

"What does Your Lordship want me to do?"

"Change places with me," the Earl said. "Then pass them, and as soon as it is convenient, draw the horses across the road and bring the carriage to a standstill."

"Very good, M'Lord."

They changed places without checking the horses.

Jason put the pistol down on the seat beside him. The Earl picked it up and looked at it, then set it down again.

"I will leave you the pistol, Jason," he said. "Hold the coachman up with it, and do not let him join in the fray."

"I'll see to him, M'Lord."

"I expect I will be able to manage the other two single-handed," the Earl said, "but if I fail, get Miss Ophelia away."

"You'll not fail, M'Lord," Jason said confidently.

Driving skilfully, he passed the carriage on a straight stretch of road.

The Earl glanced at it as they passed, and though he could not see inside through the windows, he noted that the two horses were tiring and obviously had not the stamina of his better-bred team.

The road ahead of them was empty and the Earl said after a few seconds:

"Turn now!"

Jason obeyed him, pulling the horses to a standstill, with the Phaeton across the road and completely blocking it. The carriage now following them had to draw up a minute later.

The Earl stepped down and, without hurrying, walked towards the door of the carriage.

He opened it, and the man whom he knew to be the unfrocked Parson bent forward from the back seat to ask:

"What do you . . . ?"

He got no further.

The Earl gripped him by the neck, pulled him out into the road, and hit him under the chin with the punch of an experienced pugilist.

His feet were lifted off the ground before he fell backwards and was still.

The other man, who had been sitting in the carriage with his back to the horses, was ready for action and came out the carriage door with his fists clenched, a ferocious look on his face.

Nanny had been right in describing him as a "nasty-looking fellow."

He hit out at the Earl, who dodged the blow and caught him on the side of the face.

He was tough enough to strike back, but as a fight it was a lamentable effort and he was soon laid on his back, as unconscious as the Parson.

The Earl went to the carriage and looked inside.

Ophelia was half-sitting, half-lying on the back seat.

She was gagged with a handkerchief over her mouth and he could see that her ankles and hands were tied with pieces of rope.

The Earl picked her up in his arms, carried her to his own Phaeton, and set her down. Then, climbing over her, he took the reins from Jason.

"The coachman is all yours!" he said to his groom. "When you have finished with him, release the horses."

He saw the delight in Jason's eyes as he sprang down to pull the coachman off the box, and he was as effective in knocking him out as his master had been with the other men.

Then, having first driven the carriage off the side of the road, he unharnessed the horses.

The two animals went trotting off into the nearest field.

In the meantime, the Earl removed the gag from Ophelia's mouth.

"It is all right," he said. "You are safe, and I promise you this will not happen again."

She looked at him for a moment as if she could hardly believe he was real, then burst into tears.

She hid her face against his shoulder as he undid the ropes that bound her wrists and ankles.

When she was free the Earl put both his arms round her and held her close.

"I know it was horrible," he said, "but surely you knew I would rescue you?"

"I prayed . . . and prayed," Ophelia sobbed, "and I was . . . so frightened you would not . . . hear me."

"I heard you," the Earl assured her, "and I promise that in the future I will keep you completely and absolutely safe from such horrors."

"It was . . . Stepmama who . . . sent them," she whispered, "and she will try . . . again."

The Earl was about to say something when Jason, looking extremely pleased with himself, came back to the Phaeton.

"Shall we leave them lying there in th' road, M'Lord," he asked, "or shall I shove them in th' ditch?"

"Leave them," the Earl answered. "We do not wish to defile ourselves any further by touching such scum!"

Jason grinned at him and jumped up onto the seat at the back of the Phaeton.

The Earl turned the horses, not back the way they had come but towards London.

He had taken his arm from round Ophelia, and as his team settled down to a comfortable speed, without any urgency, he turned to look at her.

She had stopped crying and was wiping her eyes with a small handkerchief which she had tucked into the sash round her waist.

"Where are we . . . going?" she asked after a moment, her voice still low and frightened.

"I am taking you to stay the night with my Great-Aunt Adelaide," he said. "She is the Dowager Countess of Tewkesbury, a redoubtable old lady of whom most people are justifiably afraid. But I think you will like her and she will like you."

"Nanny will be . . . worried if I do not . . . return."

"I will let Nanny know that you are safe," the Earl answered. "But I think my horses have travelled far enough, and from here London is nearer than the Castle."

"You . . . saved me," Ophelia said, "but I do not understand why Stepmama should have sent such strange and horrible men to kidnap me."

"I suppose no-one else would undertake such a task!" the Earl said lightly.

He had no intention, unless he could not help it, of telling Ophelia the real reason, but he had underestimated her intelligence.

"I think . . . although I might be . . . wrong," she said after a moment, "that they were . . . something to do with . . . Black Magic."

"Why should you think that?"

"I could feel how . . . evil they were. They made me

feel . . . like . . . I felt when I used to see . . . Step-mama's face before you gave me the . . . picture."

The Earl did not reply, and after a moment she said: "Would they have . . . sacrificed me?"

"Whatever they had intended to do," he replied stern-ly, "you know that now it will not happen. Forget them, Ophelia. Even to let one's mind linger on evil is, I am sure, a mistake."

"Of course it is," Ophelia agreed, "for that . . . way it might get a . . . hold over . . . me."

She shivered, and the Earl said:

"I told you, you are safe! Nothing—human or su-pernatural—shall ever harm you again. I will see to that!"

"How can . . . you be . . . sure?" Ophelia enquired.

"I will tell you a little later," the Earl replied.

She thought he was referring to the fact that as Jason was sitting behind them, he might be able to hear what they said.

She gave a little sigh which was one of happiness, and, without really being conscious of what she did, she moved a little closer to the Earl.

He looked down at her with a smile and she said:

"Is it very . . . indiscreet to drive . . . like this? I feel I want to . . . hold on to you and be quite . . . certain you are really . . . here."

"I am really here," the Earl said, "and you can thank Nanny for that."

"Nanny?" Ophelia questioned.

"She sent me a note saying that she needed me, and because I knew that Nanny of all people would not ask me to come unless it was really urgent, I left London immediately I received her cry for help. But as you know, I was just too late."

"Was Nanny very . . . upset?"

"Naturally, she loves you."

"And I love her," Ophelia answered. "I have been so happy in that dear little cottage, hearing about you when you were a boy. I would like to live . . . there for the . . . rest of my . . . life."

"I think in time you would find it rather small and restricting," the Earl said.

"It may be small in itself," Ophelia said quietly, "but it is very big with love."

The Earl smiled at her again.

He could not think of anyone who would express more eloquently what he himself had thought about anywhere that Nanny dwelt.

When he was a child she had given him the only love he had ever known and had protected him against his mother's animosity and continual fault-finding.

The Nursery at the Castle had been a place filled with love, and, although he had not realised it or expressed it in the same words as Ophelia had, that was what he had felt when he visited Nanny in her small thatched cottage.

They drove on in silence for a short while. Then when the first houses of London loomed ahead of them, the Earl turned in at two stone-flanked gates and drove up a short drive.

In front of them was an attractive red-brick Queen Anne house with long windows and exquisite stone carving over the front door.

"Is this where your Great-Aunt lives?" Ophelia asked in a nervous little voice.

"I want her to look after you and be quite sure that nothing will upset you while I have certain things to do," the Earl replied.

As Jason ran to the horses' heads, he stepped from the Phaeton, then lifted Ophelia down.

"Your Great-Aunt will think I look very strange without a bonnet," she said a little nervously.

"You look lovely!" the Earl answered, and he could see the surprise in her eyes.

She did in fact look very attractive in one of the gowns he had sent her from London, this one of pale periwinkle trimmed with *broderie anglaise* threaded through with narrow velvet ribbons.

Because he knew that she was nervous, the Earl held her hand in his, and as the door of the house was opened by an elderly Butler with white hair, they stepped into a cool Hall which smelt of pot-pourri and bees'-wax.

"How are you, Dawes?" the Earl asked.

"Well, thank you, M'Lord. You'll find Her Ladyship in the Garden-Room."

The Earl hesitated for a moment, then said:

"I think, Dawes, that Miss Langstone, whom I have brought with me, would like to tidy herself. Will you take her upstairs and ask your wife to look after her while I find Her Ladyship?"

"I'll do that, M'Lord," Dawes said, and added in a fatherly manner to Ophelia:

"Will you follow me, Miss? I'll show you the way."

He went ahead of her up the stairs and Ophelia followed him, but she looked back at the Earl with an expression in her eyes which made him want to go after her and hold her close against him.

"She has been through a very harrowing experience," he told himself, "but she has been extraordinarily brave about it."

He knew that if such a thing had happened to Lady Harriet or to any of his other women-friends, they would have been fainting or screaming hysterically, and exclaiming over and over again at what they had been through!

The Earl, knowing his way, walked across the Hall towards the Salon which looked out over the back of the house onto a formal rose-garden.

He could see in the sunshine his Great-Aunt, wearing, as he expected, a wig the same colour as her hair had been as a girl, and jewels worthy of an Eastern Potentate, without which she never would move.

As soon as the Earl opened the door, three King Charles spaniels raised their heads, then sprang towards him with a noisy greeting of yelps and barks.

"Good-day, Aunt Adelaide," he said, advancing across the room.

"Rake!" his Great-Aunt exclaimed. "Is it really you —or am I seeing a ghost? I have not seen you for such a long time that I thought you must have died!"

The Earl smiled.

"No, I am alive," he answered, "and I have come to ask a favour of you."

"I might have known you would not call without wanting something," the Countess said tartly.

The Earl raised her heavily be-jewelled hand to his lips, then kissed her cheek.

"No need to ask how you are, Aunt Adelaide," he said. "I have never seen you looking better."

"Flattery will get you nowhere, young man," the Countess replied. "I am annoyed with you, as I have every reason to be."

"I have been extremely busy," the Earl said, "and so you must forgive my neglect."

"I cannot think why I should do that."

"Only because you are the one person I can trust at this particular moment, which is why I come to you as a supplicant."

"What is it this time?" the Countess asked in a resigned voice. "If it is more emigrés, I will not have them. The last you brought me were quite intolerable. They complained about everything, and their children broke two of my best Crown Derby plates!"

It was an old story which the Earl had heard several times. He had in fact replaced the plates, which was something his Great-Aunt conveniently forgot to remember.

"The French Revolution has been over for some time," he replied.

"But France now has that monster Napoleon!" his Great-Aunt snapped. "He might be up to anything!"

"It is not the monster Napoleon I am concerned with at the moment," the Earl replied, "but Circe Langstone."

"Circe Langstone?"

The Countess's voice rose several notes and her eyes were bright with curiosity.

She would have found growing old intolerable could she not keep abreast of all the scandal and gossip of the Social World, and this, in some extraordinary way, she contrived to do.

The Earl told her briefly what had happened, and as he did so he knew that the Countess was enjoying every word of the story.

"I have heard about that woman," she said. "I hear, too, that you call her the 'Serpent of Satan.' It is obviously an extremely apt description."

"That is what I thought," the Earl answered. "And now I am asking you if you will look after Ophelia for a short time, while I make sure that this sort of thing does not happen to her again."

"How are you going to do that?" the Countess asked.

"I will tell you later," the Earl said, rising to his feet as he spoke, for he had heard footsteps outside the door.

"Miss Langstone, M'Lady!" Dawes announced, and Ophelia came into the room.

She was a little nervous, but the Earl saw that she had tidied her fair hair and washed the dust from the journey from her face.

She looked very young and very spring-like, and at the same time rather anxious and still a little afraid.

Then, as her eyes went to the Earl, the King Charles spaniels rushed towards her.

She bent down to pat them as the Earl reached her side and took her hand in his.

He drew her across the room to the window, and as they stopped in front of the Countess he said quietly:

"May I, Aunt Adelaide, present to you Ophelia Langstone, my future wife?"

* * *

A little later, leaving Ophelia with his Great-Aunt, the Earl drove back to Berkeley Square.

There was a smile on his lips which told Jason that he was well pleased with himself, but he obviously did not wish to talk and they drove in silence.

The Earl in fact was thinking of the surprise in his Great-Aunt's eyes when he presented Ophelia to her and the astonishment in Ophelia's.

Then this had been replaced with a radiance which seemed to transform her whole face.

The fear, the anxiety, and the tension were wiped away as if by a shaft of sunshine, and when she looked at him he thought it would be impossible for any woman to be so lovely.

"My dear boy!" the Countess exclaimed. "Why did you not tell me? I had no idea! Oh, I am so glad!"

"I am delighted that it pleases you," the Earl said.

"Pleases me?" the Countess repeated. "When we have all been begging you, longing for you to marry for the last ten years?"

She held out her hand to Ophelia.

"Come, child, and tell me how you have been so clever as to catch the most elusive, most infuriating, and most self-sufficient bachelor in the whole country."

"You are not to make Ophelia feel shy," the Earl said, to save her from answering his Great-Aunt. "Because she has been staying with Nanny, she thinks I am the hero of all her dreams, and I will not have her disillusioned."

"I imagine only you could do that," the Countess replied.

The Earl, with a little smile, bowed his appreciation of the shrewd thrust of her tongue.

He knew, as a light luncheon was quickly supplied for Ophelia and him, the Countess having eaten earlier, that Ophelia looked at him with an incredulous expression, as if her whole world had turned topsy-turvy and she was not quite certain what to do about it.

At the same time, her eyes told him it was almost too wonderful for her to contemplate.

Only just before he was leaving, when the Countess was being helped by Dawes back to her usual place in the Salon, did the Earl draw Ophelia into the Morning-Room and they were alone.

He did not speak but just stood looking at her, and after a moment she asked in a hesitating little voice:

"D-did you . . . mean what you said . . . or was that . . . perhaps just a way of making . . . me seem more respectable?"

He realised that this could be a reasonable explanation for what had just occurred, and after a moment he said very quietly:

"Is that what you would like it to be?"

"I am . . . thinking of . . . you."

"And I am asking you to think of yourself," the Earl answered. "It is something which, surprisingly, unlike most women, you forget to do."

"You . . . cannot really . . . want to . . . marry me."

"Why not?"

"Because you are so important . . . so magnificent . . . and you know that I am not the right person for somebody . . . like you."

"I think that is for me to decide," the Earl answered, "and you must forgive me, my darling, if instead of asking you first, as I should have done, I told my Great-Aunt, because I knew she would look after you as I wished her to do."

"Do you . . . really mean . . . ?" Ophelia asked uncertainly.

"I really mean," the Earl said, "that I want more than anything in my whole life for you to be my wife."

He thought that the room had suddenly been lit with a thousand candles as Ophelia's eyes met his.

Then with an inarticulate little murmur she moved towards him and hid her face against his shoulder.

"I am . . . dreaming," she whispered. "I did not even . . . dare to . . . pray that you would . . . love me."

"But you wanted to do so?"

"I have loved you . . . I think . . for a million years," she replied. "You are everything a real man should be . . . and yet I never thought . . . for one moment that I could . . . mean anything to you."

The Earl turned her face up to his.

"When we have a little more time," he said, "I will tell you exactly what you do mean, and how much I love you!"

He bent his head as he spoke, and his lips found hers.

He could not imagine that any woman's mouth could be so soft, so yielding, and yet so exciting.

For a moment he was very gentle, kissing her almost as if she were the child he sometimes thought her to be.

Then as he felt her press her body a little closer to his, as he felt a sudden ecstasy make her respond to his kiss, he knew that this was different, very different from anything he had ever known before.

He felt sensations rising within himself that were not only unfamiliar but somehow sacred and Divine, and yet more ecstatic, more wonderful than anything he had ever imagined a man might feel.

And for Ophelia, it was as if he filled the whole world, the earth and the sky, and she knew this was what she had always wanted, the love that she had known was part of God.

She knew that the Earl's arms gave her a sense of security and the fact that he was there swept away her fears and even the memory of everything that had made her afraid.

She felt that he lifted her into the sky, that her feet were no longer on the ground, that there was only the music of the spheres, and everything dark and menacing was left behind.

"I love . . . you! I . . . love you!" she whispered when finally he raised his head; and looking down at her face, he said:

"And I love you, my darling!"

His voice was strangely hoarse and unsteady. Then he pulled her against him and kissed her until she thought it impossible to feel such rapture and not die from the wonder of it.

She did not know at the moment that the Earl was thinking frantically that he might have lost her.

He set her free, then he said:

"I have things to do, my darling, which have to be done, but you will be safe with Aunt Adelaide, and if I do not return to you tonight, I shall be here tomorrow morning. Then we will plan how soon we will be married."

"Can it be very . . . very soon?" Ophelia asked.

"As soon as you allow me to make you mine," the Earl answered. "In fact, as soon as you can be ready."

"I . . . I am . . . ready now," Ophelia answered.

He laughed.

"You have to give me time to get a Special Licence, unless you want to be married with all pomp and circumstance at St. George's Hanover Square?"

Ophelia gave a little cry.

"No . . . no . . . please . . . not a . . . grand wedding . . . and . . ."

Then she stopped.

"What were you going to say?" he asked.

"I . . . I could not . . . bear to have Stepmama there . . . hating me."

"She will not be," the Earl said firmly. "Leave everything to me."

He kissed her again more gently, then with his arm round her shoulders he took her to the Salon.

"Look after her, Aunt Adelaide," he said. "She is a very precious person, and I cannot think of my life now without her."

He spoke with a sincerity which made the Countess look at him sharply. Then she said:

"You surprise me, Rake. At the same time, I believe you."

"I thought you would," the Earl answered. "Remember, you are the only person who knows our secret, and we trust you to keep it."

"You have trusted me in the past," the Countess remarked drily.

"And you have never failed me," the Earl answered. "But this, as far as I am concerned, is rather more important than anything else that has ever happened to me."

He kissed the Countess's hand, then Ophelia's.

For a moment they looked into each other's eyes and were very still.

Then as the Earl shut the door behind him, the Countess said to Ophelia:

"You are obviously a very remarkable young woman and undoubtedly exactly the right person for my unpredictable and, in the past, disreputable great-nephew!"

Chapter Seven

Dusk was coming in but it was not yet dark, while a tall woman hurrying down Limbrick Lane moved with a nervousness that was obvious.

There was, however, nothing in the dirty street to make her apprehensive, unless one counted an old rag-and-bone merchant collecting pieces of rubbish which he was throwing into a dirty sack.

He had long white hair hanging in a matted mass to his shoulders, and a disreputable black hat pulled low over his forehead.

In his toeless boots and a ragged torn coat which hung about him, he looked like a scarecrow.

His rickety cart, with two wheels that had spokes missing and which carried three filled sacks, stood at an angle at the side of the lane.

However, the woman walking down the centre of the road was concerned only with finding one house, and when she did so, she hurried more quickly than before up to the front door.

She knocked, the door was opened immediately, and a gleam of light flooded out into the dusk together with the sharp, acrid sweetness of incense.

The door had no sooner closed than another person came down the road, this time an elderly man, prosperously dressed but with unfashionably long hair and a beard.

He was followed a few minutes later by another, pale-faced and aesthetic-looking, who, with his hands deep in the pockets of his overcoat, was obviously ill-at-ease.

He glanced from side to side as he approached the house, then before he knocked on the door he looked over his shoulder.

The rag-and-bone man went on filling his sack.

Number 13 Limbrick Lane adjoined No. 14, which was derelict, but there was a narrow passage between 12 and 13, which enabled the owners of both houses to have a back as well as a front door.

There was a dirty path overgrown with weeds along the side of the house, and the rag-and-bone man moved there, peering through the clutter of weeds growing against the wall of the house as if in search of rags or papers that were worth collecting.

He looked at the back door, then returned the way he had come, noticing, as he did so, that the windows of the house were all darkened and no light shone through them.

More people were entering the house through the front, amongst them a middle-aged woman with the puffy eyes and relaxed mouth which proclaimed her a drinker, and a man with a military bearing which gave him an authoritative air as if he wished to rule the world.

Then for a short time there were no more visitors, until at the end of the lane a carriage came into view.

It drew up outside No. 13 and a footman with a cockaded hat sprang down from the box to open the carriage door.

A lady stepped out with an undeniable grace. She was wearing a heavy black velvet cape edged with sable and it had a hood which shadowed her face. As the door opened, it was possible to see a glint of red hair and green eyes that slanted upwards at the corners.

The carriage drove on to wait a little farther down the street, and as it did so, a woman opened from inside the door of No. 13 and looked out anxiously.

She was elderly, dressed flamboyantly in gypsy fashion with a head-dress from which hung gold coins and a necklace which glittered from the light behind her.

She looked up the lane and down again; then, obviously disappointed at not seeing what she sought, she went back into the house and shut the door.

The rag-and-bone man suddenly seemed to be galvanised into action.

Taking two of the sacks from his rickety cart, he

walked with them along the path at the side of the
house and set one sack down outside the back door,
the other under a back window.

He hovered round both sacks for a moment or two,
then returned to take the third sack from his cart and
place it firmly against the front door.

Again he seemed occupied with the base of the sack,
until, returning to his now-empty cart, he started to
push it slowly up the lane.

He had not gone far when there was an explosion
from the back of No. 13 which sounded like gun-pow-
der, and a moment later another explosion came from
beneath the window.

The third, at the front door, was louder than the
others, seeming to echo and re-echo down the lane, and
in an instant there were flames springing upwards in
the darkness.

There were more minor explosions and with them
the crackling of wood, followed by screams from within
the house, both deep and shrill.

The rag-and-bone merchant did not wait, but merely
walked rather more quickly towards the end of the lane
and vanished into the gathering gloom.

*   *   *

The Earl, changing from his riding-clothes into far
more elegant garments, was tying his crisp white cravat
in a new and intricate style which made his valet watch
him with admiration.

There was a knock on the bedroom door.

"Come in!" the Earl called, and Major Musgrove
entered the room.

"Good-morning, Musgrove," the Earl said. "Did you
have a good journey?"

"Excellent, My Lord," Major Musgrove replied. "I
cannot believe that any horses can travel faster than
yours!"

"I should be extremely annoyed if they did!" the Earl
replied.

He glanced at his valet, who immediately withdrew
from the room.

When the door closed behind him, the Earl asked:

"Did you get the Special Licence?"

"I have it here, My Lord. I also took a large number of dress-boxes to the cottage in the village, as you ordered me to do."

"Thank you."

There was a moment's pause, then Major Musgrove said:

"I have brought the morning newspapers with me, as there is something in them which I think will interest you."

"What is it?" the Earl enquired.

"Lady Langstone is dead!"

The Earl was still for a moment, then he asked:

"From what cause?"

Major Musgrove opened the newspaper he carried under his arm as he replied:

"It says here she died of an overdose of laudanum. Her lady's-maid informed a reporter that she was suffering great pain when she retired to bed and could only surmise that she took an overdose by mistake."

The Earl did not speak for a moment, then he turned to say:

"Let me see the newspaper."

"It is in *The Morning Post,* My Lord, and the same report also appears in *The Times.*"

The Earl took the newspaper from his Comptroller, but instead of reading what was printed on the front page, he turned the pages over until he found what he sought.

It was only a small item which read:

FIRE IN CHELSEA

A fire broke out on Wednesday night in Limbrick Lane where a number of people had collected to hold a meeting. It was a long time before a fire-engine could reach the house, and as panic had taken place amongst those inside the, majority of them were taken to Hospital with burns.

The only person seriously injured was the owner of the house, a Madame Zenobe, of foreign origin. She was kept at the Hospital while most of the other persons were sent home after treatment.

A lady whose face was badly burnt, a spectator reports, drove away in her carriage before she could be identified.

The house was burned to the ground and nothing that was in it was recognisable.

There was a faint smile on the Earl's face as he threw the newspaper down on the bed and returned to the position he had been in before, facing the mirror over his chest-of-drawers.

"Do you intend to tell Miss Langstone that her Stepmother is dead?" Major Musgrove asked a little hesitatingly.

"Not today, at any rate," the Earl replied, "so keep the newspapers out of sight."

"I will do that, My Lord," Major Musgrove replied. "Is there anything else I can do for you?"

"You can hand the Special Licence to the Rector who should be in the Chapel in about ten minutes' time," the Earl replied. "As I have already told you, Musgrove, you and my old Nurse will be the only witnesses of the marriage. The fact that it is taking place is to be kept completely secret."

"I understand that, My Lord."

"As my future wife should be in mourning, this gives us an excellent excuse to explain later why the marriage took place so quietly. You can send a notice to the *London Gazette* in two weeks' time, but not before."

"Very good, My Lord."

Major Musgrove went from the Earl's room and his valet came in again.

He helped the Earl into his tight-fitting but perfectly tailored coat, which, while unable to hide the breadth and strength of his shoulders, at the same time gave him an athletic elegance which made him outstanding even amongst men of his own age.

The Earl pulled the lapels of his coat into place, then left his room not through the door into the passage, through which Major Musgrove had passed, but through the communicating-door which led into the bedroom next to his.

It was an exquisite room with a huge canopied bed hung with pale blue curtains which echoed the blue in the flowered carpet and the sky behind a number of goddesses and cupids who rioted over the ceiling.

The Earl, however, was not concerned with the furnishings but with the flowers that he had ordered and which were arranged on the dressing-table and on several other tables in the room.

They were all white, all fragrant, and each vase held a different type of lily.

There was something, he thought, very symbolic in them. He knew that they not only reminded him of Ophelia but that she would enjoy them.

He left the room and went downstairs to inspect the flowers which decorated the other rooms, making the Salon particularly a bower of fragrance and beauty.

He stood at the window looking into the garden and thinking that every man, if he had a choice, would choose this sort of wedding-day, quiet, intimate, with no frivolous distractions from the solemnity of the ceremony itself.

It was, he admitted, the last sort of wedding he had ever expected to take part in.

Always he had known that because of his rank and because he moved in the fashionable world, any woman who married him would want a huge Reception to which all their friends would be invited and an elaborate marriage in a fashionable Church with the Prince of Wales as guest of honour.

The Earl now knew that there was nothing that he wanted more than to have Ophelia to himself and to know that her love for him would not be tinged with fear or nervousness but only with the wonder that he evoked in her whenever they were together.

He had not thought it possible that any woman could radiate love so strongly so rapturously that her eyes were soft and yet brilliant.

It was not the fires of desire which the Earl had aroused so often in other women, but something Divine and holy that had never entered into his life until now.

'This is different—so very different,' he found himself thinking not once but a thousand times.

When yesterday evening he had driven Ophelia from his Great-Aunt's house back to the village and handed her over to Nanny, he had known that they were both thinking, with a kind of rapture, that there were only twenty-four hours left before they would be together for always.

"You will be quite safe, my precious, for tonight," he said, "so do not be afraid."

"I am afraid of nothing . . . except that you might stop . . . loving me," Ophelia replied.

"That would be impossible," the Earl answered, "for I not only love you but find myself growing more and more in love every minute we are together."

"I feel like . . . that too," she said simply.

The Earl put his arms round her and kissed her until they were both breathless and it was an agony to have to separate even for one more night.

"Nanny says it is unlucky for me to see you until we meet at the altar," the Earl said, "and because I am taking no chances, Nanny shall bring you to the Castle, and Major Musgrove is coming down from London early in the morning to escort you to the Chapel."

"You are quite . . . sure you will be . . . there?" Ophelia asked.

"Quite, quite sure!" the Earl said with a smile.

He kissed her again, then returned to the Castle, feeling as if his whole world had turned a thousand somersaults and he was not quite certain whether it would ever right itself again.

He had never imagined in all his years of rakishness and cynicism, and mocking at what people called love, that he would feel enraptured, infatuated, and so overwhelmingly, absurdly happy that it was hard for him to recognise himself.

He could hardly believe that love could come to him so swiftly and overwhelmingly that he still could not credit that it had actually happened.

He had never for one moment dreamt that he would fall in love with the whole-hearted idealistic emotion of a boy of seventeen.

And yet that had now happened, and, being so much older, he could appreciate and savour the wonder that it meant after so many years of knowing only imitation forms of love and being satiated with them.

Before going to bed he had stood at his open window and looked out in the direction of the village, thinking of Ophelia lying in her tiny room under the thatched roof.

Tomorrow she would find herself the Chatelaine of half-a-dozen great houses filled with the treasures of centuries.

Yet he knew that fundamentally she would not alter.

She had an instinct for what were the important and right things in life, and that was something which neither possessions nor anything else could spoil.

"I love her! God, how I love her!" the Earl said to himself, and found himself longing for the night to pass so that he could see her again.

*   *   *

To Ophelia the world had suddenly become an enchanted place that was like the fairy-land she had imagined as a child.

She still could not believe that the Earl, of all people, should love her, and yet she knew that there was an undoubted link between them that was not merely human but something spiritual and a part of her prayers.

"Once I belong to him, nothing will ever frighten me again," she told herself, but she knew that belonging to each other would mean much more than casting out fear.

She knew that the Earl could teach her so much from his experience, his courage, and his hatred of cruelty, but she also had something to give him.

She told herself that she would pray every night that she would bring good, not evil, to the Castle and anywhere else they lived.

When she awoke, the sunshine coming through the window dazzled her eyes and she felt as if everything was brilliant from that moment on.

Nanny unpacked the boxes which Major Musgrove

had brought from London and left on his way to the Castle, and she exclaimed with delight over the wedding-gown.

It was very simple, and yet with its soft gossamer lace and fine muslin, it was a perfect frame for Ophelia's beauty.

There was no veil, because no-one was to know they were to be married and she might be seen travelling through the village dressed as a bride.

Instead there was a wreath of real lilies-of-the-valley, and it made Ophelia look like the Goddess of Spring, especially when in the Hall of the Castle Major Musgrove handed her a bouquet of the same flowers.

He thought, as he did so, that she was the most beautiful girl he had ever seen in his life, and he knew that the Earl had, by some amazing good fortune, found the complement to himself.

If he was magnificent and outstanding in appearance amongst other men despite his raffish reputation, Ophelia had an arresting loveliness that was spiritual and pure. This ensured the balance between them which would make them, when they were married, one complete person.

Major Musgrove led Ophelia down the long passages which led from the centre of the Castle towards the Chapel, which had been built in the oldest part of the house.

As they walked in silence she felt she ought to be looking at the pictures, the suits of armour, and the ancient flags which decorated the walls, but she could think of nothing except the man who she knew would be waiting for her and to whom her heart went out like a bird flying towards the sky.

When she came into the Chapel, the Earl, who was standing at the far end of it, felt as if she lit the whole building with an inner light which came from her soul.

Then he saw the expression in her eyes, which filled her small face, and he knew that her love reached out towards him and he felt as if his heart beat with hers.

The Rector was an elderly man who read the Marriage Service with a deep sincerity and made every word seem real and personal to the two people standing in front of him.

He blessed them at the end of the Service and Ophelia felt as if her mother blessed her too and was glad that she had found both safety and love.

There were glasses of champagne for the Rector, for Major Musgrove, and for Nanny. Then the Earl took Ophelia away to another part of the house, where there was a meal prepared for them in the Orangery.

It was a very romantic setting, for the orange-trees which had stood there for several centuries were in blossom and there were also a number of other exotic plants which had just come into flower.

"It is so lovely!" Ophelia exclaimed, clasping her hands together.

"And so are you!" the Earl said. "And this is where, my darling, we start our honeymoon towards the stars, and no-one is going to disturb us until we are ready to descend to earth again."

She smiled at him as if she were a child who listened to a fairy-story. Then he said:

"I do not think you are strong enough to travel so soon after being so ill, so I thought we would stay here at the Castle for a week or so. Then, when you are really well, we can go to one of my other houses and see if you like it better."

Ophelia laughed.

"I should be happy wherever I was if . . . you were there, but I can imagine nothing more attractive and at the same time magnificent than this!"

"I have a lot of treasures to show you," the Earl said, "but there is plenty of time for that. What we really have to do is to start exploring each other. I feel you know very little about me, and I know very little about you, except that I love you so overwhelmingly that nothing else matters."

"I wanted to . . . say that . . . first!" Ophelia cried.

As she spoke, she put out her hand to touch him, as if she wanted to be sure that he was real.

After they had eaten in the Orangery they wandered out into the garden, and under the blossoms of the fruit trees the Earl kissed Ophelia until once again she could only say that everything was enchanted and exactly like fairy-land.

There was in fact so much to talk about, so much to see, that the hours they were together seemed to pass like minutes, and almost before they were either of them aware of it, they had eaten dinner and moved from the small Dining-Room into the flower-filled Salon.

The Earl had not remained behind with his port but accompanied Ophelia, and as she stood at the open window looking out at the sunset, he asked:

"You are not tired, my precious?"

"I do not feel as if I shall ever be tired again," she replied. "You make me want to fly in the sky, dive down into the lake, and dance over the lawns!"

She drew in her breath and cried in a voice that was very moving:

"I am so happy . . . so wildly . . . unbelievably happy!"

The Earl put his arms round her.

"That is what I want you to say, my precious one, but I also have something else to say."

She looked up at him quickly.

"What . . . is it?" she asked.

"Nothing frightening," he said. "Just something I want you to listen to."

"What is it?" she asked again.

"It is this, my lovely darling. You have been through such a horrible experience and been so ill that if you are tired and would rather rest tonight, I shall understand."

She looked puzzled, and he said:

"What I am saying, my sweet, is that this is our wedding-night, and I want to make love to you and make you my wife, not only legally but actually, so that we become one person with our bodies as we are already in our minds."

The Earl paused, then said:

"But we have, God willing, many, many years ahead of us, and so perhaps it would be the sensible thing for you to go to bed now and sleep peacefully."

He knew, as he spoke, that it would be hard for him

to know that Ophelia was sleeping in the next room to his and not to open the communicating-door.

But he loved her so overwhelmingly that, for perhaps the first time in his life, the Earl was setting aside his own desires because he loved someone else more than himself.

Then as he waited Ophelia said in a very small voice:

"I . . . I think I would . . . like to go to bed now, as you suggest . . . but please . . . I would want . . . you to come with me."

"Are you sure?" the Earl asked a little hoarsely. "Quite sure, my darling?"

"I was thinking last night . . . when I was alone," Ophelia answered, "how . . . wonderful it would be to be . . . with you . . . and to be . . . close to you."

She blushed a little and hid her face against him.

"I am . . . not quite . . . certain," she went on, "what a man . . . and a woman . . . do when they . . . love each other . . . but anything you did would be . . . perfect and part of . . . God."

The Earl shut his eyes for a moment and his lips were against her hair. Then he said:

"That is what I want you to feel, my precious one."

He turned Ophelia's face up to his as he spoke, and while her lips waited for his, he looked down at her, searching her face.

"You are very beautiful, my lovely wife," he said, "but it is so much more than that. You are good and pure, and that is what I have never found in anyone before and what I have always missed, although I was not aware of it."

"I want to be . . . good for you," Ophelia replied. "Then, because we are good together . . . I know that evil will not be able to . . . hurt us."

He heard a little tremor in her voice before she went on:

"When I . . . held Saint Veronica's picture in my hand, I could . . . feel the good pouring out from it like the rays of the sun, and now . . . I can feel those same rays coming . . . from you."

For a moment the Earl wanted to reply that it was

impossible; that so many things he had done in his life were reprehensible, wrong, and perhaps even wicked.

How could he give out anything which Ophelia, in her purity, would not recognise for what it was?

Then suddenly he knew the answer: it was his love that she was feeling, and the love he had for her which was pure and good and which came from a soul that he had not really known he possessed until he knew her.

She had asked him to pray for her, and strangely, he had prayed, although perhaps that was not the right word, because even then he had loved her.

Now he knew that if Circe Langstone had not died, they would still have triumphed over the evil that she had directed towards them.

The love which was part of Ophelia, and which was now part of himself, was from God and was stronger than anything that Satan could produce.

The Earl's arms tightened round Ophelia, and with his lips very near to hers, he said softly:

"I love you, my darling, and now I am going to carry you to bed and, as you wish, we will be together tonight, and for the rest of our lives."

His lips came down on hers and Ophelia's arms went round his neck to pull him even closer.

He felt an ecstasy rise within them both and knew that it was something so pure, so perfect, that it was what he had searched for without knowing it.

He raised his head to say:

"I love you, I adore you, I worship you!"

Then, lifting her in his arms, he carried her up the great carved staircase towards the room that was waiting for them. . . .

* * *

Later, very much later that night, Ophelia whispered:

"I did not know it was . . . possible to be so . . . happy and not be in . . . Heaven."

"I want you to be happy, my precious, perfect little wife."

"And I have . . . made you . . . happy?"

"Like you, I did not know such happiness was possible in this world."

"You are so wonderful . . . I love . . . you."

"And I love you, my adorable one."

Ophelia's head was on the Earl's shoulder and his arms were round her.

He thought that no other woman could be so soft, so sweet, and so responsive to everything he had asked of her.

He had been very gentle, knowing from his vast experience that she must be awakened gradually to the wonder and ecstasy of love and that if she was frightened he might lose her trust.

But Ophelia's love transformed everything he did into something Divine, and he knew that he himself had never known such rapture as they had experienced together.

Now, as he felt that she was safe forever in his arms, he said:

"I have something to tell you, my darling."

"What is it?"

"Your Stepmother is dead."

There was silence for a moment, then Ophelia asked:

"Y-you did not . . . kill her?"

"No, she died from an overdose of laudanum. It was in the newspapers this morning."

"Is it . . . wicked of me to be . . . glad?"

"I think the world is a better and cleaner place because she is no longer in it."

"And Papa . . . will be . . . free!"

Ophelia gave a deep sigh.

"Perhaps now he will go back to being like he was with Mama . . . kind and sympathetic, and interested in . . . me. It was only Stepmama who . . . changed him."

"When you wish to do so we will tell him we are married."

The Earl knew that Ophelia was thinking before she said in a small little voice:

"Can I ask you . . . something?"

"Of course, my precious. What is it?"

"Could we go on being . . . secret and . . . alone for

a long time? It is selfish of me but . . . I do want you . . .
all to . . . myself!"

The Earl laughed.

"And that is what you have forever, my wonderful
little love—me, all to yourself, from now to eternity."

"Oohh!"

It was a sound of sheer happiness.

Then Ophelia turned her lips to the Earl's shoulder,
and as if it was the only way she could express her
feelings, she kissed it, saying between each kiss:

"I love you . . . I love you . . . I love you . . . !"

The hint of passion in her soft voice and the pressure of her mouth brought the fire to his eyes.

He lifted her face to his.

"I worship you," he said, as he had said downstairs.

Then he was holding her mouth captive and her heart
was beating against his as the wings of love enveloped
them with the Divine protection of God.

ABOUT THE AUTHOR

BARBARA CARTLAND, the world's most famous romantic novelist, who is also an historian, playwright, lecturer, political speaker and television personality, has now written over 200 books.

She has also had many historical works published and has written four autobiographies as well as the biographies of her mother and that of her brother Ronald Cartland, who was the first Member of Parliament to be killed in the last war. This book has a preface by Sir Winston Churchill.

Barbara Cartland has sold 100 million books over the world, more than half of these in the U.S.A. She broke the world record in 1975 by writing twenty books, and her own record in 1976 with twenty-one. She has also recently recorded an album of love songs with the Royal Philharmonic Orchestra.

In private life, Barbara Cartland, who is a Dame of the Order of St. John of Jerusalem, has fought for better conditions and salaries for Midwives and Nurses. As President of the Royal College of Midwives (Hertfordshire Branch), she has been invested with the first Badge of Office ever given in Great Britain, which was subscribed to by the Midwives themselves. She has also championed the cause for old people and founded the first Romany Gypsy Camp in the world.

Barbara Cartland is deeply interested in Vitamin Therapy and is President of the British National Association for Health.

Barbara Cartland

The world's bestselling author of romantic fiction. Her stories are always captivating tales of intrigue, adventure and love.

☐	02972	A DREAM FROM THE NIGHT	$1.25
☐	02987	CONQUERED BY LOVE	$1.25
☐	10971	THE RHAPSODY OF LOVE	$1.50
☐	10715	THE MARQUIS WHO HATED WOMEN	$1.50
☐	10975	A DUEL WITH DESTINY	$1.50
☐	10976	CURSE OF THE CLAN	$1.50
☐	10977	PUNISHMENT OF A VIXEN	$1.50
☐	11101	THE OUTRAGEOUS LADY	$1.50
☐	11168	A TOUCH OF LOVE	$1.50
☐	11169	THE DRAGON AND THE PEARL	$1.50
☐	11962	A RUNAWAY STAR	$1.50
☐	11690	PASSION AND THE FLOWER	$1.50
☐	12292	THE RACE FOR LOVE	$1.50
☐	12566	THE CHIEFTAIN WITHOUT A HEART	$1.50